lost
in
las
vegas

Books by Monty Joynes

Naked into the Night

lost in las vegas
monty joynes

HAMPTON ROADS
PUBLISHING COMPANY, INC.

Cover design by Marjoram Productions
Cover photo by Branson Reynolds

For information write:

Hampton Roads Publishing Company, Inc.
134 Burgess Lane
Charlottesville VA 22902

Or call: (804) 296-2772
FAX: (804) 296-5096
e-mail: hrpc@hrpub.com
Web site: http://www.hrpub.com

If you are unable to order this book from your local
bookseller, you may order directly from the publisher.
Quantity discounts for organizations are available.
Call 1-800-766-8009, toll-free.

Library of Congress CIP Number: 98-072213

ISBN 1-57174-089-9

10 9 8 7 6 5 4 3 2 1

Printed on acid-free paper in the United States of America

*To the Native American holy men,
medicine men, singers, and dancers
who hold and preserve the wisdom
of their ancestors for all humankind.*

PROLOGUE

The dawn came to the pueblo in the Rio Grande Valley, ten miles from Santa Fe, as a curtain going up on a stage. Visibility was granted in steady increments of light as the sun first outlined the Jemez Mountain peaks to the west. The two men wrapped in blankets sat against a rear adobe wall of the Winter People. It was a private place, respected as the counseling ground of the cacique, the spiritual leader of the tribe. From this vantage point, the sun rose on the men's right hand in the Sangre de Cristo mountains and set on their left hand in the Jemez.

The early day in May was cold. Snow was still seen on the mountaintops. But as the sun rose, the valley would warm so that a man working outdoors would only require a single wool shirt. The two men met each morning before dawn, usually at the cacique's wall, to see the sunrise. They did not speak to each other until there was full light. It was a discipline necessitated by their purpose. To the members of their tribe they were holy men dedicated to the spirit world. In their own awareness, they were souls clinging to

7

the Reality of the Great Spirit against the tide of illusions in the material world.

One of the men was a Pueblo Indian, a direct descendent of the Anasazi, or Ancient Ones, who lived and farmed along the Rio Grande long before the Spanish colonized New Mexico. He had become the cacique of his tribe through a long apprenticeship as a priest which had revealed his spiritual qualities. Although his Indian name and office were held secret by his tribe, and an elected Pueblo governor ran the daily business with the outside world, the cacique was the final authority in a tradition which did not separate secular from religious life.

The other man, also venerated by the tribe, but without office, was not an Indian. He had spent most of his adult years as a real estate executive in Norfolk, Virginia. In partnership with his wife, he had built a sizable business with multiple locations and had acquired significant social and political power in his community. In his fifty-fourth year, the man known then as Winston Burlington Conover became inwardly dissatisfied with the purpose of his life. Unbeknownst to his wife and two grown children, he underwent a radical transformation of his thought processes by means of self-inquiry. By accident or providential design, the man disciplined himself to observe his own thoughts, one by one, until he achieved periods of thoughtlessness. Once beyond the chatter of the mind, he recognized another reality that gave him the experience of bliss. Thinking that he must then remake himself as a human being, he had quietly undressed very early one morning and walked away from his wife, his children, his business, his home and his material lifestyle in a state of total nakedness. Somehow he had arrived fully clothed as a wayfarer in Santa Fe ten days later and had become a boarder in a primitive pueblo home because he could not afford the resort hotels. The man, now renamed Booker Washington Jones as the result of an acquired Social Security card, had been hosted by a ninety-plus-year-old woman. Booker had developed a non-verbal relationship with the old woman and had served her by chopping firewood, carrying water, and, to the amazement of the Indians, even cleaning her chamber pot. He had remained at the pueblo, finding work among the Indians with a father and son who provided cooking firewood to tourist restaurants. When the woman died some months later and was accorded a secret traditional burial high in the mountains, the man known as Booker was made a member of the tribe and of the woman's extended family, the Deer Clan, and was given the Indian name Anglo Who Became Chief Old Woman's Son. During the same period, he had proved himself a spiritual brother to the cacique.

The man left his Indian home and returned to his family in Norfolk to seek resolution by completing the life he had started there. Then, divorced and rejected as the new man, he returned to Santa Fe to practice the peace he had discovered.

And so each daybreak, the spiritual brothers, Joseph, the chief priest of an ancient religion, and Booker, the remade modern man, sit together in a silent bond they would extend to all people.

*lost
in
las
vegas*

CHAPTER ONE

When Winn Conover arrived as Booker Jones on the Pueblo reservation, he had stood out as a wayfaring anglo with his stubby white beard and backpack. But after months on the desert plains harvesting mesquite and piñon firewood with Ernest Silva and his son Carlos, Booker was bronzed like them. As full-blooded Indians have little facial hair, Booker took to shaving his face as a gesture of merging with the tribe. Months after completing his life in Norfolk, his silver gray hair hung down his back in a single ponytail. On feast days Maria, his Deer Clan sister, would insist on braiding his hair so that two tightly woven braids hung behind his ears and fell across his shoulders. Whether working on the mesquite plains or sitting with the elders of the pueblo beside the blanket-covered arbor which protected the statuary carried from the Catholic Church on the day of the Corn Dance, Anglo Who Became Chief Old Woman's Son was indistinguishable from the rest of his Indian family.

Anglo, normally a derisive term when applied to tribal outsiders, was spoken with reverence when it applied to Anglo Who Became Chief Old Woman's Son. The tribal family had witnessed the subtle transformation of the holy man. Certainly he had lost weight and strengthened himself physically since coming to the pueblo, but there was more. There is a way an Indian man carries himself when he walks in the natural world of his ancestors. Great warriors had this carriage, this presence. Anglo, unconsciously, had assumed the posture, the carriage, and the walk of a realized Indian man. The stride was confident, yet fluid. The man walked with purpose, yet he required neither mankind nor nature to be disturbed by his passing. Heads turned, and perhaps even leaves and flowers leaned into his presence, in recognition of the harmony and power that he represented.

It is said among Indian peoples that certain medicine men can become invisible because of their direct connection to the natural world. A medicine man collecting medicinal herbs for his curative teas and compresses talks to the plants, seeking the permission of the chief plant to gather what he needs. If he requires the flowers of a bush thick with feeding bees, he also tells them of his need and asks them not to sting him in the performance of his harvest. If the medicine man confronts a hostile snake or a mountain lion, he gives the animal assurances of respect and passes unharmed. Occurrences that seem magical to non-Indians are accepted norms to Native Americans who practice the old ways. They live within another reality, a reality that Anglo entered one careful step at a time.

But there are few medicine men left among the tribal nations and few caciques to pass on the essential legacy of their reality. In some tribes of the late twentieth century, tribal councils are already dominated by half-breeds who seem more concerned about finances than preserving their spiritual heritage. They have the white man's disease in their blood, other Indians say. They have lost the vision that only pure-blood Indian eyes can see.

Joseph was concerned by the lack of candidates within his own tribe who could carry the essential secrets into the next generation. The tribe had once been a strong people; it had had Rio Grande Valley habitations since 1300. But after two rebellions against the Spanish, crop failures, and a smallpox epidemic that killed half the people in the late 1700's, the tribe was passed by treaty to the anglos, whose treatment drove the remaining population into further poverty and despair. By the mid-1990's, a reservation of over 25,000 acres could claim tribal membership of only 900 people. Fewer than 300 lived in the pueblo itself, and many were only daytime residents who operated shops or came on tribal business. At night the TV screens and inside flush toilets beckoned. Only the old, traditional people remained to feed the dogs and guard the unseen treasures of the pueblo.

Among the few tribal young people, Joseph searched for a leader who could carry his spiritual mantle. There were six men in his priesthood to officiate at ceremonial rituals, and Carlos Silva, when initiated, would be a seventh. There were the elders from both the Summer and the Winter People, who carried much wisdom in the crevices of their weathered faces. There were also serious singers and dancers in the tribe, who kept traditions like the Corn Dance and the Animal Dance and who could be depended on to participate. Pearl, Nita's successor as Chief Old Woman, and Maria would continue to lead the women and the girls in the old ways. But where was the chosen one? He was not among the tribal politicians who coveted the silver-headed cane presented by President Lincoln to Pueblo leaders in 1863, seeking its power and authority. It seemed that they all wanted to become white men.

There had been one bright hope, however. A boy who loved the drum, who sang well, and who danced even from childhood with amazing skill and intensity. For Joseph's tribe, ritual dances were a very important spiritual expression, perhaps more important to them than to any other tribe among the Indian nations. As the best dancer, Ramon Ortiz was accorded great honor. At Giveaways to celebrate the achievement of a son or daughter, Ramon always received the most valued gift. Had the tribe not been so poor, Ramon would have been a rich man in gifts recognizing him as the head dancer.

As a teenager, he danced the most important ritual roles. He was a prodigy, a humble, beautiful man-child who seemed dedicated to the tribal heritage. The entire tribe rejoiced in and celebrated his talents.

But at age 15, Ramon had been lured away to show his prowess at powwows across the Southwest. He first adapted his skills to Grass Dancing, a style of war dancing that required quick foot movement, agility and balance. There were ever-present older dancers and drum groups to offer transportation to the obviously gifted newcomer. At powwows handsome dancers attract Indian princesses in throngs. They are the centers of attention, and those in their company have ready access to the girls who surround them.

Although no drugs or alcohol are allowed at powwows, the parties that spill over into the campgrounds and nearby bars are also the stuff of Indian legend. Indian families travel hundreds of miles to attend powwows. Time and distance are not relevant.

Many Indian young people have their first drink of alcohol and their first sexual experience beyond the lights of the dance circle. That powwows produce pregnancies is common knowledge and the subject of ribald Indian humor. Young

Ramon Ortiz was soon assimilated into this moveable feast of fry bread, ancestral drum, dance competition, and intertribal carousing.

There are over 1,000 powwows in North America every year. Native American drums, groups of 8 to 12 men who drum and sing for the dancers; dance competitors; and vendors of beads and buckskins and books and tapes crisscross the continent to supply the demands of heritage.

Ramon went on the powwow trail as soon as his ninth grade school year ended. He had only his mother to please in this request, and then he was on the road. At first, he congregated with the Grass Dancers to learn more about his craft. He danced cautiously and respectfully from the end of May to early September with only one third-place finish to provide eating money. Food, transportation, and even beer seemed plentiful to him although he had little or no money to contribute. His growing circle of friends on the powwow circuit didn't seem to mind.

"You will win some prize money," they told him. "Then you can pay."

By nature, Ramon was shy. He had been taught respect for his elders and nearly everyone he traveled with or met at the powwows was his elder. He was also a virgin. If he feared the intensity of the Grass Dance competition performed before audiences that sometimes numbered in the thousands, he feared the attention of lustful girls more. He could not imagine what he would say to them or how he could look into their faces. His bashful demeanor seemed to make the young women more aggressive, but they were picked off by Ramon's entourage before they could get close to him.

A wise elder who had instructed Ramon in the movements of ritual dance had told the boy, "Dance and understanding will come." Even in the first summers on the powwow trail, Ramon relied on his dreams for inspiration and lit sweetgrass as a purifying incense in whose smoke he bathed his hands and face. The pow-wow competition songs were sometimes tricky, and he once or twice over-stepped the final drumbeat and disqualified himself. Older compet-itors smiled at the mistakes of the intense Pueblo brother, while at the same time realizing that he had the qualities to be a champion.

In his second summer, Ramon placed in the major powwows he attended and won most of the smaller ones. He attracted notice and began to be invited to larger and larger events. At 17, his third year in competition, he won every Teen Boys Grass event and became its Champion of Champions. In his last year of high school, he competed as a Junior Adult, an 18-to-30 age cat-egory. The next year he won enough competi-tions to earn over $30,000 and was considered one of the best Grass Dancers in the nation.

But Ramon was already spending his money on a Fancy Dance regalia and practicing with the Southern Style Fancy Dancers. Champion Fancy Dancers were the superstars of the pow-wow world. Their costumes were the most elaborately beautiful, with double bustles, feathers, ribbons and bright streamers swirling wildly as if the dancer were aflame. The dance itself required great athleticism and stamina. It was a burst of pure energy which held an audience suspended until the freeze frame of the final drumbeat. Then they exploded in waves of appreciation as if the energy expended by the dancers could be returned by the release of cheers and applause.

But Ramon, although a powwow-weary professional at age 20, was still a purist when it came to dance. He danced with dignity and with such skill that his feet barely touched the ground. He was of the Earth and yet he seemed to float above it like the sacred eagle. The power and the glory of the body magnified until it scintillated the essence of light itself. This is why Ramon danced. He danced to be transcended. The spirit and the body merged for moments of ecstasy. Perfection was attained. The discipline achieved in those performances was what Spanish kings and American governments could never extinguish: Divinity.

An observer could mistake the purpose of Fancy Dancing. The men could be viewed as peacocks performing for esteem and for the highest prize money. Certainly dancers saved their best moves for the championship rounds, but only the pure of heart could reach the heights of endurance and beauty that inspired awe. Only the transformed could reach the heights of eagles.

In the days before the world fell on their culture, young warrior dancers would fast for four days in preparation for the Corn or Animal Dance. On the day prior to the ceremony, small groups of dancers ran 20 miles in the four directions and performed rites at appointed sacred places. Then they started back, running another 20 miles to the pueblo to dress for the dance. Finally, they danced forty minutes of every hour for six hours. Only then could they eat and rest. This was Ramon's tradition. This was why Joseph viewed the boy, now man, as the future spiritual leader of his diminishing tribe. And when Ramon won the National Championship at Schemitzun, the Mashantucket Pequot Tribe Powwow in Connecticut, in a year that earned him over $50,000 in prize money, Joseph hoped that Ramon would come back to the reservation and begin the process of becoming the cacique. But months passed and finally the news arrived: Ramon was lost in Las Vegas.

CHAPTER TWO

In the kiva, where the elders and priests taught the few young men who were returning to the old ways the songs of the drum, Anglo was also instructed. The music at first seemed beyond Anglo's comprehension. It seemed dissonant, a kind of yelling with the voices often strained and rising into falsetto. There were songs, many songs, in the tribal language and others sung as vocables. Their lyrics were simple statements to be sung no less than four times, and then repeated until the head singer gave a subtle vocal cue to end the song on the next repeat. Singers and dancers listened for this cue during intertribal social dances, contests or ceremonials, so that they could stop abruptly on the final beat of the drum.

The traditional songs, sung in the four languages of the Pueblo Indians, seemed simple when translated into English. The song, sung in chant-like repetition, takes on a life of its own. The drum becomes, in those moments, a unifying heartbeat that resonates through all participants.

The singing becomes trance-like, transportive in spirit as the body exercises supreme focus. And the same occurs with the dance, whether it is the stately shuffle of Traditional Straight Dancing or the wildly exhausting spinning of the Fancy Dance. The drum circle unites and uplifts all who enter it with honor and respect. For Anglo, the drum, the singing, and the dancing were passports to Divine meditation. He took to them with all the energy and emotion his being contained. Joseph had never seen such a devoted novice in his kiva.

Carlos Silva, the young man who had once bet his father that the anglo could not get up at sunrise to work with them in cutting mesquite, and then had made a whole-life's commitment to apprentice himself to the priest council, naming Anglo as his guide, ran in his dreams to keep up with his elder. Carlos knew many of the songs popular to his tradition. He and his father, Ernest, often sang when they worked in the desert. But to sit in a firelit room with Anglo, keeping time with a hand drum as the two men sang a song that Anglo had only recently learned, was like hearing the song again for the first time. Two or three nights a week, the anglo and the Indian boy who honored him met in the kiva to practice the songs Anglo was learning. It was not unusual to sing the same song for a hundred or more repetitions. Some nights they sang a single song for nearly three hours. It produced the sweetest exhaustion Anglo had ever felt. He could not conceive of native singers who could sing for ten or twelve hours at a time.

As Anglo found his drum voice and began to sing the vocables of the intertribal songs full throat, the private sessions attracted hearers to the wall of the kiva. The back is considered a spiritual receiver to Pueblo Indians, so to sit or stand against the kiva wall while Anglo and Carlos drummed and sang was to experience the intensity of their devotion. There had not been such nightly inspiration in the silent pueblo for many years. In the darkness of the plaza, the sounds vibrating beyond the kiva made ancient echoes among the adobe walls. As more people came to listen, there were only spaces remaining for the latecomers to stretch out their hands and touch the wall with their palms.

When the drum ended, the people dispersed like shadows, not wishing to disturb the wholeness of the event, not speaking, only leaving behind some item of food or drink to replenish the singers when they came outside.

The first time Anglo was taken to a powwow he came upon the gathering of tribes in a dusty field full of cars, campers, tents and teepees. A large tent with open sides exposing the backs of bleachers was at its center, and at the center of the circle within the tent was the drum, or to be more specific, three drums, surrounded by singers and their families sitting on folding chairs. With the exception of the drums, one a Cochitis-made cottonwood shell covered with bullhide, the presence of the coolers and the small children playing on a blanket made the circle seem like a picnic site. But, although the other drums were commercial bass drums, each was regarded as sacred. Each had an individual personality, a given personal name, and each was in the care of a specially appointed guardian. The singers of each drum were devoted to their instrument as a means of creating a lifting energy which moved them to another level of consciousness. Every person in the circle who sang, or danced, or placed focus on the drum experienced deeper realms of the Self.

While the ten or twelve men who sat around a drum applied their soft-headed beaters in slightly accented 2/4 time, the head singer began the first phrase of the song. Then the other singers began, repeating the phrase and then entering into the entire song. Near the end, the head singer began the introduction phase again, overlapping with the other singers as they drew to an end. As long as the head singer did this, the song was repeated. Otherwise, the other singers and the dancers knew that it was the last time through.

Anglo learned that Southern drums, especially Sioux drums, use a drum cue. On the last time through, the singers strike the drum more softly, in unaccented beats, then build to a loud climax on the final beat. The signal could be as short as five beats or as long as nine.

In ages past, when Native Americans depended on each other for trade, powwows were week-long affairs. Different languages were not a barrier to singing together. Indians believe that the songs unite them with the past and create a continuum through the present into the future. The sounds themselves have healing and revealing qualities. Meaning is revealed directly through bodily vibration. To overcome the language barrier, familiar songs are sung as vocables such as aah, eh, oh, ee, and uu.

Indian music so confused the white men who first encountered it that they believed it to be tonal gibberish without merit. The voices quavered in tremolo. The tunes sounded off-key. Witnesses called it devil music. Even musicians trained in western musical notation could not document it. The western scale could not accommodate the notes. Indian music used more notes. It was a multi-toned scale more akin to Oriental composition. What early reporters wrote off as primitive nonsense was actually a very sophisticated art form of complex rhythms, with singers often in counterpoint to the drumbeat. The singing was done in unison, not in harmony. Indian music today still sounds very dissonant to the western ear.

Anglo, however, was prepared for its strength and power. He felt the alignment of spirit becoming form in the character of the drum. The chant-like nature of the songs, sung in repetition after repetition, brought together the physical, emotional, mental and spiritual bodies. Harmony was achieved out of unison. He sat on an old wooden bleacher for hours as each drum took its turn. He saw the singers lose themselves to the expression of singing as the drum became a bridge across time. All ancestors seemed to have their voices carried on the drum's vibrations. Anglo listened for the wisdom of the ages, and by this surrender he entered into the circle with all who sang and all who danced.

His first powwow did not include competitive dancing. It was an intertribal social dance for every member of the family. Many dancers wore dance regalia, but many men and boys danced in blue jeans and boots or sneakers, with only a turtle shell or gourd rattle to keep time with the drum. Women without traditional fringe or jingle dresses danced with a blanket or a shawl across their shoulders. Children were unrestrained and moved freely among the dancers as they circled the drum in a clockwise direction. Some were costumed and appeared to have undergone instruction. Others, smaller children, were just doing their best to imitate their elders.

After the first five hours of drumming and singing and dancing, with pauses for Giveaways and Honor Dances where families and friends accompanied the honoree in a Round Dance around the Circle, the powwow took a break before the evening Grand Entry and another session of intertribal dancing that would go on past midnight.

Anglo, accompanied by Carlos and Ernest, made the rounds of the food concessions and vendors positioned around the central tent. The first order of business was to try the fry bread. There are many, many different ways to say fry bread in Native American languages. The item itself seems simple enough: water, flour and salt that is rolled and molded into shape and then dropped into hot oil. But tribes hold fry bread cooking contests every year, and Indians are always on the lookout for the perfect piece of fry bread.

"What do you think?" Carlos asked his father after the men had taken a bite.

"She could cook in my teepee," Ernest said with a wink to Anglo.

Anglo purchased an Indian taco, a small, plate-sized piece of fry bread wrapped around ground beef, grated cheese and salsa, with shredded lettuce. The Silva men wrapped their fry bread around thick Buffalo sausages covered with cooked onions and green peppers.

"Let's take some black medicine," Ernest suggested.

Carlos saw Anglo's confusion. "He means let's get some coffee."

There were a surprising number of vendors for such a small powwow of maybe 600 people. Some vendors simply displayed their wares on blankets. Others had blanket-covered tables and standing wooden backdrops for displays. A few had pop-up canopies where their crafts were arranged on tables.

The most numerous items for sale were turquoise and silver jewelry pieces. Second were the vendors of cassette music tapes. There were three types of tapes offered: Native American flute recordings by artists like Kevin Locke, Carlos Nakai and Douglas Spotted Eagle; Northern Drum songs by such groups as the Blackstone Singers, Black Lodge Singers, Cree Singers, Common Man Singers and Elk's Whistle; and Southern Drum represented by groups such as Southern Thunder, Fort Okland Rambler and MGM Singers. Some music vendors also offered books on Indian subjects and instructional videos on native crafts.

Since most dancers make their own regalia, there were vendors with feathers, furs, hides, beads, bells and old snuff lids used for rolling into jingles for jingle dresses. There were tin cones and sinew thread; leather thongs; metal-backed mirrors; bone and horn hairpipes; horse and bull tails; earth paints; porcupine hair roaches; botanicals like sweetgrass, desert sage and osha root; feather fans; rattles; reproduction eagle feet; bear claws; grizzly, wolf, buffalo, and elk teeth; fox and other tails; and coyote faces.

Anglo had never seen such things apart from the complex regalia of his own tribe, and then only on ceremonial days.

There was also a Hudson Bay Point Blanket vendor. Dating back to 1779, the 100% virgin wool loomed blankets were originally traded for beaver pelts during the expansion of the Canadian Northwest. They are still made in England and presented in gift boxes. Anglo had seen them generously distributed at Giveaways. He never imagined that they were such a costly gift. Four-point blankets sold for $180 while the six-point blankets were $225.

Another vendor had Taos-made hand drums. In sizes from eight to twenty-four inches in diameter, the drums were built from bent wood frames. When a frame was finished, wet rawhide was stretched over one or both sides of the hoop and laced to the frame.

Anglo tested one of the drums with a beater. It had a deep, rich tone. Perhaps it was time for Anglo to have his own hand drum. Then when they practiced in the kiva, Anglo could keep time with Carlos's hand drum. Both Ernest and Carlos were consulted, and several drums were tested. Anglo paid $100 for a single-sided 16-inch drum. His joy was immense. Ernest and Carlos walked behind him as Anglo kept checking the bag to make sure the drum was still inside.

"He is like a reservation kid with a new bi-cycle," Ernest observed. "He won't believe it is his unless he can sleep with it."

"Let's buy him a t-shirt," Carlos said with en-thusiasm. The shirt that they bought was a black shirt with a deep green and purple design of a warrior with a bear-claw shield. The design was based on ancient Indian rock art called petro-glyphs. It was immediately Anglo's favorite gar-ment.

CHAPTER THREE

It was a warm, sunny day when Vincent Delgado passed through thick adobe walls into the subdued light of the kiva. He had never faced a private gathering of his tribe's Elders, and he was nervous.

Vincent had been away from the reservation most of his young adult life, traveling the pow-wow circuit as a crafts vendor. He was not a craft-maker himself, but an important middle man for individual makers of painted pottery, plaited yucca baskets, carved wooden deer dancer figures and Kachina dolls, who were scattered among the pueblos around Santa Fe. Vincent was a competent merchant who owned his own truck and might have made a good living except for the excesses which required him to carry three fictitious driver's licenses a year for the ten speeding tickets that he averaged every 50,000 miles of interstate driving.

Vincent, being unmarried and in his mid-twenties, was also known to consume mass quantities of beer and liquor after the powwow business day, and to be the special friend of Fancy Dancers who could always catch a ride in his truck or enjoy his beer and food cache when their pockets were empty. There was a method to Vincent's generosity that earned him a name among powwow travelers. He was called Fox Trap. Where Fancy Dancers were handsome of face and beautiful of body, Fox Trap was pockmarked, big-nosed, squat and beer-bellied. Nevertheless, when the young women came to party with their heroes, the Fancy Dancers, Fox Trap somehow always managed to fill his bed.

Generally, Fox Trap was an outgoing, unusually expressive young man, but on entering the tribal kiva of the famous cacique, Joseph, his head was downcast, his posture submissive. Vincent did not practice the old ways, but he was not able to ignore the summons of the Elders whose medicine was still considered powerful.

The old men sat in a broad circle at the center of the kiva room. Some sat together on crude wooden benches, while others had individual chairs or sat on backless leather camp stools. A vacant chair stood on the perimeter. Joseph gestured for Vincent to take the seat. No one spoke. Although the Elders were not in ceremonial dress, six of the eight men around the circle had a feather fan or a rattle in their hands.

"Welcome," Joseph began. "Your Grandfathers have asked you to come into our lodge so that we may know the condition of our son, White Wing."

Vincent had seldom heard Ramon Ortiz's tribal name spoken. On the powwow trail, Ramon was simply known as Dancer.

Joseph went around the circle and named the Elders, who were acknowledged individually by Vincent. "And this is Anglo Who Became Chief Old Woman's Son," Joseph said.

Vincent had heard about the anglo who had been adopted into the Pueblo tribe, but he had not believed the stories passed from reservation to reservation and powwow to powwow. Some said the spirit of Nita, Chief Old Woman, had passed into a white vagrant at the moment of her death and that the white-bearded man had disappeared for months, only to return to her house as a smooth-faced, darkened brother. The man who sat on Joseph's right hand, positioned in the Spiritual North, indeed looked like an Indian. Vincent's eye twitched when the anglo spoke a greeting to him in his own language. "So," his mind concluded. "The anglo is real."

"Tell us of our son," Joseph requested.

"He is working in Las Vegas," Vincent began. "I stayed with him four days last month."

"Tell us what you saw. Tell us all," Joseph said when Vincent hesitated.

Vincent knew what was required. He could not lie, or embellish, or deceive. He was expected to

be their eyes and their ears. It was a duty too
ingrained by tradition to deny.

"Dancer—Ramon—I mean White Wing, is Fancy
Dancing in a big casino review at the Tropicana
Hotel. He does two shows a night. He comes on
in what they call a production number with
showgirls and dancers. He only has to work his
specialty number and then he comes back for
the final thing with everybody on stage. He goes
to work about seven for the seven-thirty show,
takes a break before the late show, and is free
a little after midnight. For this they pay him
$600 a week. Living is cheap in Las Vegas.
Dancer's got an apartment better than a good
motel that he shares with only one other guy.
You can run the air-conditioning all day and all
night. The light bill ain't nothing because they
make the electric cheap at that Lake Mead Dam.
And you can eat plenty, all you want, at the
buffets in the casinos. Four bucks at midday and
you ain't hungry the rest of the day. And
Dancer, he don't get up until two or three in
the afternoon. He lives at night like an owl.
White women are always asking him out after
the show. Two of the showgirls are his special
girlfriends. Sometimes he stays with them, but he
likes to play the games, too. He likes this game
'Let-It-Ride.' It's like poker. At a bunch of tables
they know Dancer, and we get all the free
drinks we want. No more beating the road for
Dancer. He is the National Champion Fancy

Dancer and Las Vegas wants him. That's how he got the job. The producer saw him win the title at the Schemitzun Powwow. They gave him a contract and paid his expenses to Las Vegas. It was his first time in an airplane. Maybe he will be a movie star, but he don't forget his brothers. There is always a blanket on the floor for whoever comes."

"Who is his drum?" one of the Elders asked.

"He don't need singers," Vincent explained, "they got a big orchestra on tape that sounds live. It plays music written just for Dancer's number."

An Elder shook his rattle as if to dispel a pesky insect. The others did likewise.

"Does he purify?" another Elder asked.

"Grandfather," Vincent said, "you can't burn no sweetgrass in the dressing room. Those white people are crazy against fire. You can't even smoke tobacco."

"We hoped White Wing would return to his people after he became the Grand Champion," a third Elder said. "Did he not earn a lot of money?"

"With respect, Grandfather," Vincent began, "White Wing won every contest last year, but a good powwow only pays $1,000 for the top prize. The money gets you to the next powwow. It allows you to have a motel room instead of a tent. It allows you to repay past favors and to support brothers who did not win prize money. Even the $5,000 he won at Schemitzun didn't last long. He had to celebrate, didn't he? The Foxwoods Casino was next to the powwow grounds. You have to give something back to your hosts. The Mashantucket Pequot Tribe owns the casino. That's how they are able to pay $750,000 in prize money. That's why we go to Connecticut for the National Championships. The Champion drum wins $30,000, but even that is not a lot of money when you pay expenses and divide what remains among 12 singers."

"Does White Wing practice the white's religion or does he keep the old ways?" an Elder asked.

"From what I see, Grandfather, he practices no religion. There is a Paiute reservation near Las Vegas, but White Wing don't go there. I wanted to go out that way to see Mouse's Tank in the Valley of Fire, but he was too busy."

Joseph turned to Anglo to comment. "Valley of Fire is a holy place. The ancient ones, our own people, cut pictures into the red sandstone in the sacred valley 3,000 years ago. Mouse was a Paiute hunted by the whites. Mouse's Tank was a secret water place. They would chase him into the Mojave Desert in the Valley of Fire but when their water ran out, they could not stay to catch him. Today our holy places are a State Park."

When there were no further questions, Fox Trap was presented with a six-point trading blanket and thanked for his visit. The Elders did not discuss what he had told them. They would wait three days that would be devoted to sweats and fasting before they would come to any conclusions. They would purify themselves, seek a vision on how to proceed, and then they would decide what to do about their lost son, White Wing.

CHAPTER FOUR

The fire in the sweatlodge was begun at dawn by the younger priests, assisted by Anglo, who provided fragrant woods from the Silva stockpile. As the ancient stones in the pit heated, a process that would take until early afternoon, Joseph received two of the oldest Elders in his adobe house. He knew that they came on a matter of great importance; otherwise, they would not have interrupted his, and their own, preparation for the sweat.

"We are troubled," one of the Elders began.

Joseph nodded and the three men took chairs around a small table.

"We were silent when the anglo was given a tribal name and adopted into the Deer Clan. We were silent when the anglo sat with us beside the arbor for the Corn Dance. We kept our peace when the anglo came into our sweatlodge and entered the kiva to learn our songs. All these things we have accepted. But now the anglo is included in our sacred council. Tomorrow we dance the Kachina and seek our vision for White Wing. These things no white man, no outsider has ever seen. In our lifetime we have killed our own brothers who spoke these secrets outside our people. How is it now that we open our kiva and our holy ways to this man?"

Joseph was silent for more than a minute, then he spoke warmly and with confidence, looking into the face of each man. "The Hopi tribal priests have been the storehouse of our ancestral visions. They foresaw that our tribal nations would fall to their knees, but that we would not perish from the earth. The prophecy says that white men will finally come who will understand us, appreciate us, join us; and by them, we will be saved and multiply. I believe our people can fall no further. The prophesied white men must therefore appear. I believe that Anglo Who Became Chief Old Woman's Son is one of these men."

The two Elders sat in silence. A tear escaped at the corner of one man's eye.

After a long silence, Joseph spoke gently. "Let us sweat with our Anglo today and look into his heart. You can then decide if he is worthy to enter our sacred council and see the Kachina Dance. We must be in agreement."

The sweat was long and purifying. At some point for each participant, the rational mind ceased to function and a vision-inducing trance objectified another reality. It is in this altered state that Indian peoples seek Divine guidance.

The insights do not come without individual devotion and discipline. Joseph and the Elders had
trained their entire lives for these moments.
Anglo had come to them by desperation, surrender, and finally something called luck, or destiny.
He had stopped to observe his own mind, one
thought at a time. So when he arrived as a
boarder in the simple adobe home of Nita, Chief
Old Woman, he was ready to learn within her
Silence.

Following the sweat, the old men were helped
up the ladder onto the roof of the sweatlodge.
There they were given water to revive them, and
the sweat was scraped off their skin with long,
curved antelope rib bones. With blankets thrown
over their shoulders each was supported to his
own house, where he would dress and prepare
for the dawn of the third day, at which time
decisions could be made.

The three Elders representing the Turquoise
moiety of the Summer People, and the three representing the Squash or Winter People, entered
the kiva from the east where Joseph and Anglo
awaited them. The Turquoise men had their bodies painted in broad black and white horizontal
stripes. They represented Koshares, masked gods
who ensured the well-being of the pueblo. The
Squash men had their bodies divided vertically,
one half painted white with large black spots
and the other half painted yellow ochre. They
represented Kurenas, another group of protective

gods. Both Koshare and Kurena were considered invisible spirits of the deceased.

All of the Elders wore ragged black breech-cloths, strips of rabbit fur on their wrists and on their moccasins, and belts of deer hoof rattles at their waists. Each man carried an eagle feather fan in his right hand. They entered on a drum-beat provided by a priest sitting in the center of the room, and began to sing as they circled him. The song ended when they had positioned themselves in the south, where benches were provided for them to sit.

Joseph then produced a short elbow pipe made from decorated pipestone, filled it with to-bacco and lit it. The priest who had beat the drum took the pipe to each participant, who smoked it in turn. Then from a flat, rectangular cottonwood box, Joseph removed six very old Kachina dolls, one for each of the six Elders. As the drum began anew, each Elder rose in turn to dance his Kachina around the circle. As he danced, holding the Kachina up in his right hand and the eagle fan in his left, he sang intently. There seemed to be no time frame or set pattern to the individual dances. It was as if the man were searching in a time outside of time. The drum ceased only when the Elder stopped and stood silent. Then each man addressed the coun-cil about the nature of his vision.

"In the long ago," one began, "my Kachina was brother to the Twin War Gods. He was a warrior who protected the people. Where are the warriors now, he asks? Who will dance to celebrate my victories? Who will sing my love songs and play my cedar flute? Who is worthy of my memory? Who can dream my dreams? Run to his lodge. Search for him in the river valley and the mountain woodlands. Follow him into the desert. Do not let him forget his people. I cannot live unless he remembers me."

Another Elder concluded his dance and spoke. "My Kachina is guardian spirit, given at birth with the soul by the Mother of All. He carries a prayer stick that will admit the soul to Shipap. Some of us will return to our pueblo as rain clouds and make the crops grow. Corn Mother will rejoice. But now there are fewer and fewer souls to guide to the Underworld. And of these, few are qualified to enter the innermost world to become rainmakers. My Kachina wants to enter a great soul who will nourish our Mother. He is troubled. Many seeds are put into the ground, but there is almost no perfect corn. Only perfect seed can produce perfect corn. Find my perfect seed, he says. Water my perfect seed."

A third Elder spoke. "My Kachina speaks like a coyote. He is lazy and wants to make mischief. He finds us thirsty and stops on the trail before us, turning his head as if asking us to follow. But instead of leading us to the water, he takes us into the desert. Coyote sings us to sleep and then steals into camp and eats our only bag of corn. Coyote imitates us, but we cannot consider it flattery. We do not howl at the moon when there are important journeys to make."

The fourth Elder said that his Kachina was a runner. "He has run the uphill Snake Race and proved his stamina. He has been called Antelope Chief, and he has danced with poisonous serpents. But now he has run far and lost the track. A snake has bitten him, but he has no Hopi medicine to rub on the wound. He asks that we send another runner to find him, an uphill runner who can race from far below the mountain to the Joshua trees on top. The swift bringer of the medicine will receive eagle prayer plumes and a gourd of sacred water to place in his cornfield."

The fifth Elder identified his Kachina as a Soyoko, a terrifying ogre who visits the homes of naughty children. The tradition is that the ugly monsters threaten to carry off the children and eat them if their behavior does not improve. The parents then save the children by ransoms of food. The Elder spoke, "My Soyoko is out of season. There is a time for frightening children and old men into good conduct. Such moral tricks have no sway once young people leave the reservation. Can a grown son return home out of fear and threatening? No. Soyoko cannot be sent."

The sixth and last Elder finally danced and then spoke.

"My Kachina is barefoot. His hair hangs loose. His hands are empty. His eyes are vacant. His heart is a lonely hunter. He cannot speak for himself. He cannot hear the songs of his people. He asks without breath, who will find my moccasins? Who will braid my hair? Who will put my hands to work? And who will love me and bring the stars back into my eyes? Our people cry out who cannot hear and cannot speak. Who will be their ears? Who will speak for them?"

A long period of silence was observed after the Elders had spoken, and then Joseph spoke.

"Blessed are we who heed the words of our ancestors as revealed through our Elders. We feel our son, White Wing, is important to our people. We cannot consider that he is lost to us. We must reach out to him. We must bring him back to the old ways that have sustained us through so many trails of tears. White Wing has a role to play in our continuation. So say I."

"So say we," the Elders said in chorus.

Joseph turned to Anglo, who had sat silent at his side throughout the ritual. "I ask you now Deer Clan brother, Anglo Who Became Chief Old Woman's Son, to go to Las Vegas and to do and to say those right things that will restore White Wing to his people."

Anglo's hands slipped off his lap where they had remained in meditative repose. His facial expression changed from serenity to shock. His mind thundered and flashed like the energized threads of a sudden summer storm.

Joseph and the six Elders waited for Anglo's answer. Anglo seemed to be looking far away. Then he finally spoke in a slow, dreamlike voice, "Las Vegas," he said. "Profane time. Profane place."

CHAPTER FIVE

When Ramon Ortiz—White Wing—commonly called Dancer, arrived in Las Vegas, he felt as if he had been transported into a surreal world. Although he had traveled hundreds of thousands of miles criss-crossing North America on the powwow circuit since he was 15 years old, and had seen many cities, he had never ventured beyond the comfort zone of his Indian amigos. In the early years, he had slept in a tent or on the floor of a van or truck in the powwow campground. He had taken his meals at the concession stands or made simple sandwiches from bread and lunch meats purchased on the road. Later, as his talent was recognized, he was often invited to eat with powwow families whose teepees or RV's had all the comforts of a real home.

But mostly Dancer ran with young, unmarried people who seemed to have a rage to live outside of the white man's domain. If they went to bars, they wanted the room to be filled with Indians. If they stayed in a motel, they wanted to be grouped together. Wherever they went, they positioned themselves as islands of resentment in a sea of suspected prejudice. Many among them deliberately alienated non-Indians, especially whites, as if to seek revenge for the atrocities of the past. The posturing said, "I won't live in your world. Do anything you want, I no longer care." Unfortunately, the bravura was really a projection of hopelessness which led to alcoholism and a kind of depression known only to those who have experienced genocide against their kind.

So Dancer had traveled extensively in the western United States and Canada, had even seen the east where there are tribal names without a people, but he had really not experienced the dominant late-twentieth-century American culture and society. He was still a reservation Indian.

If Dancer thought that his first airplane ride was adventuresome, his entry into Las Vegas show business proved to be an immense roller coaster of provocative tests. From the moment he signed the contract and was separated from the protective environment of the powwows, Dancer had to cope with a completely new set of circumstances every day, seemingly every moment. His only asset was his physical presence, the walk of a warrior. His inscrutable chisel-faced expression, when coupled with long silences and perfunctory responses, made him appear confident,

if not haughty. It was an ancestral facade. Behind the stoical mask was a frightened boy-
man struggling to find a path through an
uncharted wild.

The Tropicana comped Dancer for three days,
in which time he was expected to attend show
rehearsals, work with the costumer, find a place
to live, and undergo an insurance physical and
drug testing. The Folies Bergere show was under-
going one of its five-year revampings and there
were new members in the 50-member cast who
accompanied Dancer in his orientation. The show
had originally been imported from Paris and had
been playing in Las Vegas in one form or another for over 35 years. It was actually a dino-
saur that depended on elaborate tableau scenes
featuring topless showgirls and dancers. Going
topless was not required, but it paid an extra
$50 a week. The old Tropicana stage still de-
pended on 20 stage hands, or flymen, who
worked the rail where they pulled ropes to raise
and lower scenery that was counter-balanced by
bars of lead weights. Most, if not all, of the
other stage shows in Vegas had already gone
high tech. No one was pulling ropes at the
MGM Grand or at Bally's, although showgirls and
dancers were still prominent. Shows like Siegfried
& Roy at the Mirage billed themselves as "The
Ultimate Spectacle" and spent upwards of $100
million making it so. Runs for such shows were
listed as "indefinite."

Because of his good looks and novelty, experienced women in the cast offered to help Dancer get settled. One dancer had a brother who was a casino dealer. He was looking for a roommate to share expenses in Paradise Village. The apartment complex on Paradise Road was just off Tropicana Avenue, and only a mile and a half from the Casino itself and Las Vegas Boulevard, The Strip. Dancer could see the aircraft parked at McCarran International Airport from the Casino rooftop. Paradise Village was also near the University of Nevada-Las Vegas via Harmon Avenue. Dancer could walk to UNLV basketball games. If Indians took to any white man's sport, it was basketball.

Jack Menendez took Dancer in for a commitment of $250 a month. "You got to pay your own phone bills and clean up after yourself" was his only admonishment.

The girls in the revue showed Dancer the red crosses on the stage floor to mark the lines where scenery dropped. "You can get hurt around here if you are not careful." They told him to focus on the exit sign above the door down the center aisle when performing. "That way, you know you're center stage and you'll always have your head up." Finally, they introduced Dancer to the various inexpensive casino buffets where he could eat all he wanted for $4 to $7 a day. For a boy raised on Bureau of Indian Affairs commodity foods, casino buffets were unimaginable feasts.

"Don't go overboard," one of the showgirls warned him. "If you gain too much weight, the director will give you two weeks notice to take it off. Of course, you can always wear some cheater weights at the first weigh-in. That way, you can show immediate losses the first week." The same girl, Kim or Holly or Lisa or Sue or Debbie—he had difficulty matching the names to the seemingly same faces—told him that her Irish mother had told her to never date men with blue eyes or to ride a light-eyed horse. It was one of many things that the girls said to add to his confusion those first days.

At the rehearsals, Dancer at first wore his own regalia and performed his own competition dances. He had to learn the entrances to his feature spots, how to hit his marks on the stage, and then how to exit without tripping over his fellow performers. Once the basic blocking had been learned, the choreographer began the refinements. Dancer had some difficulty with the mock-Indian orchestrated music written for Native Fever, his specialty number. It did not possess the soul or rhythm of a native drum with its intense singers. In frustration, Dancer played a drum tape for the choreographer during a rehearsal break. The man, who had been a dancer on Las Vegas stages for more than twenty years before becoming a choreographer, seemed perplexed by what he considered chaotic screaming. Halfway through the song he dramatically waved both hands for surcease. "Fine, fine, fine," he proclaimed. "That's your way, and I'm sure it works for you. But this is my way. God knows we paid enough for the arrangement. So let's do it as it is written. You can get it. Your dancing is wonderful. It's exciting. All you need to do is keep it in time with the score. Trust me, Ramon. It is Ramon, isn't it? Be a trooper, Ramon. Work at it. It will be OK."

In the final week of rehearsals, the director, the choreographer, and the costumer began to pick away at Dancer's regalia.

"We need to see more thigh," the director complained.

"The boy has got a beautiful set of buns," the choreographer encouraged. "Why not show 'em?"

Day by day, substitutions were made to Dancer's regalia. Surrounded by the costumer and her assistants, and prodded by the director and choreographer, Dancer was unable to stop their assaults. Off came the leggings. Then his own breechcloth was replaced by a smaller, flimsy fabric that revealed too much of his biker shorts when he spun and jumped. When the shorts were found objectionable, Dancer faced the final humiliation of being fitted with a kind of silk panty containing a cup in which to place his privates. It was the male version of a G-string which left his entire behind exposed when he danced.

As dress rehearsals ended, Dancer was almost used to seeing the bare breasts of beautiful girls who had formerly worked around him in sweatshirts. And since none of the cast members seemed to notice his partial nudity or their own, Dancer himself began to lose self-consciousness when in costume.

Backstage one hectic afternoon, Dancer was relieving himself at a urinal in the men's dressing room when one of the showgirls came in and proceeded to do the same in a doorless toilet stall. "We're full-up on our side," she explained. "There's no privacy in show business, honey. You better learn that right now."

CHAPTER SIX

Since Anglo had returned to the pueblo following the divorce settlement in Virginia, he had lived the simple life of a monk. There were few ripples of Winn Conover's life to disturb him. The Indian Reservation was his sanctuary, a refuge where he felt no poverty or self-denial. In Norfolk and Virginia Beach, although he had the advantages of affluence and social position, he had felt trapped, even hunted, by the avaricious society around him. Its pressure had driven him literally out of his mind into an awareness beyond patterns of thought. His family, looking at his subsequent behavior, had judged that he was unbalanced, even crazy. Ultimately, they had rejected him as a husband, and as a father. But the same mindlessness, the gentle unjudging, was welcomed among the Pueblo Indians as the sign of a significant human being. Anglo, like the best of them, lived each day in the fullness of itself, perceiving the expression of Reality in all things. In the Pueblo Indian's languages there is no word for the English concept of religion. There is no separation between everyday experience and spiritual experience. Every act of work or play, of seeing and hearing, is a metaphor for what stands behind it as its animating or creating Power. Being in harmony with the Power, the Great Spirit, is the very act of living.

The man called Anglo felt that he had escaped the non-reality of profane time and profane place, but now the tribal Elders were asking him to re-enter it. In the experience of Winn Conover, Anglo could recall Las Vegas, and he did not want to go there again. He felt unprepared for the mission to rescue White Wing. If he had been unable to save his own son, Theo, from the falsity of the material world, how could he hope to alter the direction of a stranger?

Winn and Ellen Conover began their gambling junkets to Las Vegas in early 1975, the trip materializing as the thoughtful gesture by some country club friends after a Greek Line cruise ship suddenly gave up the Caribbean trade and sailed silently for Greece instead of picking up passengers in New York and Norfolk, leaving its customers just two days short of island paradises. Because it was their first extensive vacation since starting their real estate firm, Winn and Ellen were in turn infuriated, frustrated and finally depressed. The invitation to join their friends on a Las Vegas junket was a lifeboat in an unhappy storm.

The friends, triple-A-rated junket players, were

able to get the Conovers included on a charter flight to the Las Vegas Hilton with only a week's notice. Generally, new junket players must be recommended by established junketeers. As first-timers, Winn had to deposit $3,500 with the Norfolk casino rep before he and Ellen boarded the charter flight. By the time they arrived five hours later, they had a $3,500 line of play established with the Hilton, which they could draw down by signing a marker at any craps table, roulette wheel, blackjack or baccarat table, or at the casino cashiers. Unused portions of these funds would be reimbursed prior to the return flight, but the house expected junket players to give them a lot of gambling action in the meantime. Failure to do so would reflect badly on the sponsor and the Norfolk rep, and keep the Conovers off any future junket invitation lists.

In flight was a five-hour cocktail party hosted by the casino rep. Acquaintances were made easily in the festive atmosphere. Complimentary decks of cards were passed out, and Winn and Ellen got plenty of free advice on how to win at blackjack and craps. Introductions were very informal. "Keep your cool," their friends advised. "If you see your lawyer or doctor with a young buxom beauty who is not his wife, look the other way. The unwritten rule is that we never mention names outside our junket crowd. And never, never talk about anybody's winnings or losses."

At check-in, Winn was given a VIP card as identification for drawing down his front money. The card also entitled him to a complimentary room, meals, beverages and entertainment for his entire stay. Some of the experienced and higher rated junket players ordered completely stocked bars and platters of fancy hors d'oeuvres from room service as soon as they got into their rooms. Ellen was timid with her first order; she had a bottle of Pouilly-Fuisse sent up. It was $22 on the room service menu. But she could have ordered anything she wanted, anytime she wanted. It seemed unbelievable to them. Chateaubriand at five in the morning, brought on a white tableclothed cart by a white-gloved waiter who served the dinner and poured the wine before leaving their room? No problem.

Charlie Rich, country music entertainer of the year, was in the Hilton Showroom. Mort Sahl, B. B. King, and Kenny Rogers were in other, lesser venues, where continuous entertainment was provided until 4 a.m. Ellen was disappointed. Ann Margret and Elvis were the next two stars scheduled for the Hilton Showroom. She had missed seeing Elvis by one week. But there were exciting alternatives. Frank Sinatra was at Caesar's Palace and Dean Martin was at the MGM Grand. Who else was playing that week? Glen Campbell, Paul Anka, Juliet Prowse, Jan Murray, Sandler and Young, Buck Owens, Foster Brooks, The Platters, The Fifth Dimension, Engelbert Humperdinck,

Totie Fields, Jerry Vale, Wayne Newton, Leslie
Uggams, Phylis McGuire, Frank Gorshin, Jim
Nabors, and Charo, not to mention the production extravaganzas like MGM's Hallelujah Hollywood, Lido De Paris, Spice On Ice, Casino De
Paris and a play, "Mind With the Dirty Man,"
starring Phil Ford and Jane Kean.

"We couldn't possibly see all the big shows if
we did two a night for a week," Ellen lamented.
"And look who is following Dean Martin next
week, it's Johnny Carson!"

While Winn was learning the multiple bets on
a craps table from his junket sponsor, Ellen alternated buckets of quarters at slot machines
with forays into casino shopping areas, where
she discovered fine furs, California designer fash-
ions, and jewelry that she had never seen in
shops in the mid-Atlantic states. It seemed a
wonderland to her.

They dined at nine that evening in the hotel's
finest gourmet dining room. For the first time in
their lives the Conovers ignored the prices and
ordered anything they wanted from the menu
and the wine list. Their hosts and sponsors were
joyfully extravagant. The meal and the service
were unequaled in the Conovers' experience, and
so was the bill, which approached $450. The host
happily signed for the tab and left a crisp, new
$100 bill on the table as a tip.

"Since we're VIP's and comped," the host reminded Winn, "the waiters knock themselves out

to get the big cash tips. We can afford to be generous, and they know it."

The two couples went to the 10:30 p.m. Charlie Rich show and then the men gambled until nearly 2 a.m., while the women played the slots for awhile and then went up to their rooms. Neither couple would be out of bed before 10 a.m. when they first stirred to order a room service breakfast.

The days in Vegas merged into a continuum of gambling sessions, extravagant meals, star-studded shows, and alcoholic libations punctuated by fewer and fewer hours of sleep. It was a fantasy whirlwind that Winn and Ellen could hardly believe once they were back in Norfolk. When Winn cashed out, they had lost all but $400 of their $3,500 deposit, but it didn't matter. The vacation had been worth it. It might have cost more, they rationalized, if Winn had not played conservatively and won a few hundred dollars along the way. They also might have come back with more if Winn had not given cab drivers twenty-dollar bills for five-dollar fares.

"How could I?" he asked Ellen. "When I cashed in my chips before we dressed for dinner, they paid out in the fewest number of bills. If you cash out $940 in chips, they give you nine hundreds and two twenties. I never saw a five-dollar bill the whole time we were there. And the driver said he had no change."

"They are never going to have change," Ellen chided. "I guess we can be glad that you had a twenty instead of all hundreds."

Money didn't seem to have the same value in Las Vegas as it did in Norfolk or Virginia Beach. Winn learned quickly how a $20 bill folded in the palm of his hand, and transferred in a handshake to a show maitre'd, could move his party from a table in the back of a showroom to a vacant celebrity booth up front. Whereas Winn Conover, the conservative business man, might drive across town to save $20 on a new set of automobile tires, Winn the junket gambler would tip a dealer the same $20 on leaving the table after winning $200, although he was down $2,000 since arriving in Vegas.

One hectic trip, after Winn was an established junket player going to Vegas at least twice a year, he lost slightly over $5,000 on his casino credit card. Arriving back in Norfolk late Sunday night, he got to his office Monday morning to find a message from the local casino rep.

"Sorry about your bad luck, Winn," the junket organizer said when Winn returned the call. "I've got your markers here, and I'd like to know how you want to handle this. Can I send one of my people over to your office this morning?"

"I'll need to go to the bank," Winn said.

"Sure," the polite collector replied. "Would you like one of my people to go with you?"

"No, thanks," Winn managed with composure. "I'll slip out around lunchtime."

"So we could pick it up about one o'clock," the rep said as a statement.

"Fine," Winn replied.

The very large man who appeared with Winn's actual Las Vegas markers in hand at exactly one o'clock could have been a professional football linebacker, a heavyweight boxer, or an actor playing a Mafia hit man.

"Talk about organization," Winn related later to Ellen, "they must have picked up the markers in Vegas and brought them on the plane last night. This morning they are already collecting."

The money that Winn lost on that particular junket would have purchased that year's XKE model Jaguar sports car. It amounted to the annual average income of many Americans. The loss nevertheless did not deter Winn and Ellen from further junkets. It was not the losses that finally ended their urges to go back to Las Vegas. It was rather the changes in the city itself. Over the years, Las Vegas became less exclusive. People no longer dressed for dinner and the shows. The entertainment became diluted by other gambling centers like Atlantic City. Too many bussed-in players flooded the casinos. The places seemed to have lost their aura of class. Cheap buffets replaced the wonderful restaurants they had enjoyed in the seventies. Junket players were monitored and even graded. Gone were the totally comped junkets unless you were a significant high roller. It was an era that had passed. Las Vegas was now for the masses.

There was a time in the life of Winn Conover when he thought that Las Vegas symbolized everything that he had worked for: privilege, pleasure and extravagance. At least for a few days a year, Winn and Ellen could have the illusion of the great wealth and excess to which they aspired. Las Vegas seemed to confirm their position on top of the heap. They considered junkets there as living life to the fullest.

But what had been a culmination to Winn was a nadir to Booker, and now to Anglo. Las Vegas represented the antithesis of his wants and desires. There was nothing in and of that place that a person should need. It was only relevant for those who worshipped Pleasure.

CHAPTER SEVEN

Dancer was a cultural hero when he walked among his own people, but on the streets of Las Vegas he was a dark-complexioned, ethnic face who was to be avoided. Yet on the sidewalks of The Strip he was also a wide-eyed tourist, just like the better-dressed people who passed him. One exception, however, was that he could run 40 miles in 24 hours if he had to. They barely managed to walk from the Hacienda to the Sahara, and then exhausted, caught the Strip Trolley back to their hotels.

There are nearly 30 casino hotels on The Strip. At night, the moving montage of neon lights, people, and vehicular traffic assault the senses to the point of overwhelming them. Every aspect competes so much for attention that people stumble into each other and even walk into the paths of oncoming taxis. They lose contact with their feet. On the sidewalks, vendors behind temporary tables gesture with colorful T-shirts. Other street people, who have the appearance of the desperate, attempt to force on passersby booklets featuring semi-nude women on their covers. They press the material on a man even if he is accompanied by a woman who appears to be his wife. Inside the covers, the color photos are more sexually explicit. They promise that the lady of your choice, white, oriental or black will come to your hotel room to perform totally nude entertainment. The advertisements also offer bad boys, transsexuals, and two girls at a time. XXX rated. Credit cards accepted. Even Dancer understood blatant prostitution when he saw it. He must have run a gauntlet of ten or more groups of sex peddlers on one pass down The Strip. The booklets pandered to sexual fantasies and invited the public to ignoble vices. To accept the offering of the booklets was to titillate the human libido into wantonness. Like a pubescent child who discovers forbidden pornography, Dancer hoarded the booklets and carried them back to his apartment for closer scrutiny.

On the street in front of the Mirage Hotel and Casino, Dancer witnessed the eruption of a mechanical volcano which turned waterfalls into rivers of fire. Next door, at the Treasure Island Hotel and Casino complex, he saw an English warship under sail do cannon broadside battle with a pirate ship, which appeared to sail up a streetside waterway. The English ship won and the pirate ship sank, with its captain on deck, into the lagoon. Such illusions, albeit in lesser productions, had convinced non-technical people all over the planet of western man's superiority. To Dancer, it was the most wonderfully bewildering entertainment he had ever seen. He made a mental note to show these things to everyone who came to visit him.

During the weeks of rehearsal for the new Folies Bergere show, the cast members had little time for socializing. They had to be available most of the day whether they were on stage or not. Dancer relieved the tension surrounding the Tropicana's Tiffany Theater by walking The Strip and seeing the interiors of the various casinos. Like a patient hunter, he was content to be an observer of the terrain—watching, watching until he understood the meaning of its shadow. He watched to see how the games were played. He watched the dealers and the players who betrayed their positions with malleable expressions and body language. Dancer concluded that none of them could be successful in the Indian game where a man must conceal in which hand he holds a stick.

Dancer took most of his meals at the casino buffets. Food that had seemed so incredible to him the first times that he saw it began to lose its appeal. For the most part it was bland to his taste or too salty or overcooked. There were enough fresh fruits, breads and meats, however, to keep him coming back. Occasionally Dancer was lured into casino restaurants for meals that seemed like fantastic values. He ate a steak and

lobster dinner with baked potato, broccoli,
fresh baked rolls and a bowl of soup for $7.95.
The steak was from an old, unhappy steer, he
judged. The lobster tail had been in a freezer
for months, and the broccoli had been raised
with chemicals and then cooked to death. Even
the soup and the white flour bread were un-
satisfying to his taste. He finally found a restaurant that he liked at the Frontier. Tortillas
were hand rolled and cooked in a window at
the front. Mexicans, who understood his Spanish, cooked their traditional meals and waited
on the tables. It was a noisy, festive place that
reminded Dancer of a powwow feed for contestants. He became a regular there. It was a
place he could bring his friends and feel welcome. He blended in with the Hispanics. He
spoke their language. He even had a Hispanic
name.

The new Folies show opened without incident
and played to over 10,000 customers the first
week. Dancer was nervous, but confident for his
performances. He prepared himself mentally in
the same way he had prepared for championship
competitions. He only lacked the purification of
the burning sweetgrass smoke. The physical demands of his four appearances on stage hardly
caused him to break a sweat, so the director required Dancer to oil his body—especially his legs
and buttocks—for effect. Several of the playful female cast members offered to help him with the

oiling. "I think I just made our Redman even red-
der," one of them told the others.

After the first week of two shows a night,
the 7:30 dinner show and the 10:30 cocktail
show, staging adjustments were finalized and
the show got into its professional routine. Cast
members now had more time to relax and explore their off-hours options. One of the preferred options for the showgirls and dancers
was fraternizing with the customers. The house
encouraged the girls to mingle with patrons between shows. Often the encounter was little
more than posing for photographs with a glee-
ful table of convention goers. Sometimes a girl
would join a table of junket gamblers during
dinner before the early show. Although she
generally did not eat or drink, she was a welcome addition to the party. If she was asked
for a date, she might accept, provided that she
accompany her escort to the gaming tables.
Her loyalty was to the Tropicana. Her hope
was that a big spender would share part of
his winnings with her. It was amazing how
generous a middle-aged man could be with a
beautiful showgirl on his arm. On a lucky
night in the casino a girl could make more
than she could on stage in a week. Sex was
not part of the deal, but it always seemed like
a possibility to the candy men. Some of the
girls formed mutual aid cliques to share bene-
factors who came in multiples.

"Debbie and I have dates after the show," Sue said, as she approached Dancer backstage between shows. "Do you want to join us?"

Dancer did not know how to respond.

"It's not kinky!" she said, in response to the blank expression on his face. "There is a woman in the party. She's the vice-president of something, and she's divorced. She saw you in the show last night and couldn't stop talking about you, so I said you might come out with us tonight."

"Where would we go?" Dancer asked simply.

"To the tables. We go along to bring them luck. They have tons of money. One of the pit bosses told me that they are triple-A players. Come on. We'll have a few drinks and they will give us chips to play along side them. Take one of every four and slip it into your pocket. We can't lose. And if they win, we will get a bigger tip than the dealer. It's easy. You might go home with a thousand bucks. We've had nights when we made two or three."

Dancer paused, trying to understand what Sue was saying.

"Come on baby," she said in a coquettish pout, "do me this favor."

"OK," Dancer agreed.

"Wear a sports coat and nice pants," she said, as she tried to depart.

"I don't have a sports coat," Dancer said.

"Damn," Sue said. "I have to do everything!"

By the time Sue and Debbie came for Dancer

they had borrowed a navy blue blazer from Security and a white turtleneck jersey from Wardrobe. After they had dressed him, Sue was still not satisfied.

"The jeans will work with the blazer. Marlboro man type thing. But the Nike's have to go. We've got to find some dark socks and a decent pair of shoes," she said to Debbie with urgency. "Give me your shoes," she ordered Dancer, "and wait right here. Don't move."

The two showgirls' high heels clacked down the hall. Dancer saw their behinds accentuated by the short, tight dresses as they went away. A few minutes later, pulling at the tops of their dresses to keep their breasts from falling out, they clacked back to him with a pair of snake-skin boots.

"It's all we could find to fit," Debbie said to Dancer, trying to catch her breath. "They belong to Bobby, the assistant stage manager. He's not real happy about the trade."

"We'll give 'em back tomorrow," Sue said tersely. "We'll put a twenty in each toe. That should make him happy."

When Grace Profitt saw Dancer approaching with Sue and Debbie, she nudged her junket buddies and said, "I feel like Ava Gardner in *Night of the Iguana* with her beautiful native beach boys."

Grace was almost 50, a little overweight, but still attractive by virtue of hair dye and carefully applied cosmetics. She wore tasteful, expensive clothes as befitted her executive status at a large furniture company that her father had founded. She was accustomed to getting whatever she wanted in a world that from childhood had seemingly centered on her.

"Ramon," Grace repeated, when Sue made the introductions, "you look like a movie star."

Dancer smiled enough to reveal his perfect teeth.

"It says on the program that you are the National Champion Fancy Dancer," Grace continued. "I've never seen Fancy Dancing before, but I find it fascinating."

Dancer could only manage a polite, "Thank you."

"What is your tribe?" Grace asked, trying to make conversation.

"I am of the Pueblo people in New Mexico," he replied.

"Near Santa Fe?" she asked.

"Yes," he said.

"I've always wanted to go there," Grace said, but the statement did not draw a response from Dancer.

"The boys want to play craps, but I've got a better game for us," Grace said. "Do you know how to play stud poker?"

"A little," Dancer replied.

"Good. We're going to play a game called Let-It-Ride. We can sit at the table together. We don't play against the dealer or any other player. It's easy to learn," Grace said as she took Dancer by the hand. "We'll see you guys and dolls later," she said to the others, and led her trophy away.

At a Let-It-Ride table, Grace signed a marker for $1,000 and started Dancer off with $250 in $25 chips. "Watch me a couple of times until you get the idea," Grace instructed. "We can't show our hands to each other when you start to play."

In the game, each player places three equal bets within his own circles on the table. Three cards from a single deck are dealt to each player and two cards are placed face down in front of the dealer. Each player is trying for the best poker hand by using his three cards and the dealer's two down cards. Winning hands are a pair of 10s or better. After looking at their first three cards, each player may take back one of the three bets or "let it ride." One of the dealer's down cards is then turned up and each player can take their second bet back or "let it ride." The dealer's second down card is turned up and the players lay their cards down, face up. The dealer then pays all winning hands according to the payout schedule. The pair of 10s or better pays 1 to 1. Two pair, 2 to 1. Three of a kind, 3 to 1. A full house pays 11 to 1. A straight flush, 200 to 1. And a royal straight flush pays 1,000 to 1.

Grace began with two $25 chips in each of her three circles. She matched up a Jack in her hand with a dealer's Jack and collected $50 on her single standing bet.

"We're ahead already," she said grasping Dancer's forearm. "I knew you'd be lucky for me."

As they began to play, Grace ordered drinks. "What do you want, Ramon, Honey?"

"I don't know," Dancer said in his inexperience.

"I bet you'd like a Margarita," she suggested. "Bring him a Margarita straight-up and I'll have a Dewar's and water."

Dancer got caught up in the poker game and played well enough to keep his original stake and improve it by over $150, playing $25 chips in his three circles. Grace was up two thousand dollars at one point during the hours of play, but then lost her original $1,000 and signed a second $1,000 marker before they left the table after 2 a.m.

It seemed that every time Dancer emptied his drink a fresh one appeared at his elbow. The tequila and lime juice had a refreshing taste, and he lost count of how many he drank. It must have been more than he was used to, because he seemed to care less and less about Grace touching his arm or leg, or kissing him on the cheek whenever either of them won a hand.

When Dancer tried to return his stack of chips to Grace when they went to the cashier, she said, "Don't be silly, Honey," and he put the four $100 bills into his jeans without protest.

Grace led him by the hand to an elevator and

then down a hotel corridor to her room. It was a suite of two rooms.

"Do you want something from room service?" she asked. "We could get champagne, shrimp cocktail, steak, whatever you want."

"I don't need anything," he answered.

"Good," Grace pronounced as she disappeared into the bedroom. Dancer stood exactly where she had released him, at the center of the parlor. He stood silently there until she returned in a silk, feminine pajama top that hinted at her nakedness above its thigh length. She came close to him and pulled his head down to where she could kiss him deeply on the mouth. He tasted the scotch whiskey on her breath. He felt the beginnings of his own arousal. He was not a virgin. He had slept with one Indian girl four times on the powwow circuit. She was sweet, and they had love for each other, but her path, her parents, took her in a direction that was not his. Later, he had been under the blanket with another, older Indian woman, who had required much of his strength to please her. He knew the body of Indian women, but he did not know anything about white women.

Grace Profitt took Dancer by the hand and led him to her bed. He did not speak, but he thought, "Now I will experience the body of a white woman."

CHAPTER EIGHT

Pueblo Indians of the once nearly extinct Pojoaque tribe were threatening to forcibly close Highway 285, the major road out of Santa Fe which ran across their reservation. The fight was over Indian gambling casinos. The tribal governor said, "We are willing to die or go to prison to protect Indian gaming." Pueblo Indian tribes had signed compacts with the New Mexican Governor to put casinos on their reservations. The Pojoaque tribe promptly borrowed $30 million for their Cities of Gold casino. Without a casino license, they could not have borrowed enough for a two-room schoolhouse. But then the compacts were struck down by the New Mexican Supreme Court because the state legislature had not been consulted on the deal. The U.S. Attorney then ruled that the tribes had to close their casinos.

Nationwide, there were 150 Indian gaming compacts in 24 states. The tribes used the proceeds to fund education, care for the elderly, support reservation infrastructure improvements and fund their own police departments. In New

Mexico alone, 3,000 jobs and $200 million in annual revenues were at stake.

Each tribe in the Rio Grande Valley recognized that the case was just another in the long history of the United States breaking its treaties with Indians. As far as the tribal political leaders were concerned, the state had no jurisdiction over their tribal lands. They were each a sovereign nation.

Anglo could not help being aware of the crisis, but he was troubled about the casinos themselves. It seemed to him that casino development on the reservations would seriously compromise the Indian way of life that had been so meaningful to him. If the young people took jobs there and were caught up in the excesses and moral vacuousness, how could the spiritual traditions of the tribe survive? Joseph agreed and told him that traditional tribal members were not in favor of the casinos.

"Casino riches are a false promise just like gambling itself. A few make money, but most will lose. Look at the placement of reservations themselves. Some may be near a major highway or not too distant from a big city, but most are in barren places that the whites did not want. If you build a casino on every reservation, many will only have Indians as their customers."

"What about the future of the tribes?" Anglo asked.

"Many tribal nations have been destroyed. They exist only in name and in the spirit of their ancestors. Other tribes have no full-blooded members. Some do not even contain half-breeds. And yet they claim reservations, form tribal councils and keep superficial traditions. They want to believe that they are of the People, but they have lost the secrets of our ancient powers. They say they practice our religion, but we have no religion. Religion is a white man's concept. It does not apply to our relationship to the Great Spirit. Even among our own Pueblos there are those who marry outside of our blood. They merge into the culture and the religion of the many, and we become fewer and fewer. Our tribal Governors honor the caciques and they say that they serve and protect us, as well as the Elders who carry the ancestral treasures in their hearts. But they covet the power and wealth that they see in the white man's casinos. They like to say that they will make the white man pay back at the gaming tables what he has taken from us. That only implies a bitter heart. They say our young people will have jobs and that the reservations will prosper. But when I look up into the mountains for rain clouds to water our fields, I cannot believe that a good crop will come from the planting of a corrupt seed."

In the Indian way, Anglo was not expected to make a decision about going to Las Vegas hastily. He spent the first day in silence, alone, and then he went back to his job helping Ernest and Carlos harvest firewood. Knowing that White Wing was of the Deer Clan, Anglo asked Carlos what he knew of his tribal brother.

"We grew up together," Carlos told him. "Ramon's father died in a car wreck before we were in the first grade. His father had a drinking problem, you know. His mother cooks good, and most of the time she has a restaurant job. She lives in a trailer closer in to Santa Fe. She comes to our house for dinner sometimes. My mother is her first cousin, so Ramon and me are close in blood."

"What was he like as a child?" Anglo asked.

"Ramon is shy. He stays within himself. Very intense. We learned the tribal songs and dances together, but it was clear to the Elders that Ramon was very special. Because he had no father, he became every father's son, especially among the old people. When we wanted Ramon to play basketball or to go rabbit hunting, we had to look in every Elder's lodge on the reservation. He would be somewhere among them, learning a ceremonial dance or sewing on his regalia."

"So he was withdrawn?" Anglo suggested.

"No, not really," Carlos recalled. "Ramon may be quiet, but he is strong. He liked to run with us. He was one of our best basketball players. We had better intertribal games than the local high schools. Our best players were better than

the whites who won college basketball scholar-
ships."

"Why didn't you play on the high school
team?" Anglo asked.

"We played for our own people," Carlos tried
to explain. "It was one of the ways left to show
yourself a warrior. It was not meant for the
whites and their rules. If you have never seen
us play basketball, you have never seen basketball." Carlos smiled a smile that showed off his
brilliant white teeth. "And we have the scars to
prove it."

"What happened when Ramon started dancing
at powwows?"

"He was our pride. Even after he won his first
championships at the big powwows, he came
home the same Ramon. He was always a serious
person. He would not get drunk and get into
trouble. He always had time for the Elders and
still danced the honor roles in our ceremonials.
Some of our boys want to be warriors, but there
is no opportunity to prove themselves in the old
ways. So they steal a car the way a young buck
used to steal a horse from another tribe to show
his daring. They do a thing, like steal beer from
a store, that gets them in trouble with the police. It is said that nobody on the reservation
was ever a kid. But White Wing came close. We
say that he is a man who never dropped an
eagle feather, a perfect Indian man. There are
men among us who feel that they have nothing

left to lose because they cannot turn back toward tradition and so they drink and they fight. They fight each other over nothing, and they pick on anyone who seems to mock them by caring about anything. You would think that Ramon would be a natural object for their anger, but he is not. I have seen drunk Indians, even from another tribe, start to abuse Ramon because he was not drunk like them, then suddenly stop with their fists in the air when another brother recognized Ramon. All the brother had to whisper was, 'This is Dancer, man,' and the fists would open into handshakes. It's like Catholics who could never hit a priest. Even a drunk Indian will not harm his last hope."

"Will White Wing come back?" Anglo finally asked.

Carlos considered. "I guess we took that as his destiny. We thought that Ramon would become a champion on the powwow trail, bring us great honor, do the prancing and bucking that young elk and good ponies must do before they can lead a herd, and then return and stay as the keeper of our ancestral ways. But now I am not sure.

"His face will break apart with a smile when he learns that I have gone into the tribal priesthood. It was not expected. I have no great talents. I have only the advantage of staying near to the reservation, of eating Nita's piki bread as if it was a Communion wafer, of sitting with my father at Joseph's fire, and finally of seeing the value of our sacred life reflected in you, a dreaded anglo. My place has always been near the fire. It has protected me through every bitter winter and from every fang of the hungry wolf. White Wing is now far away from the warmth of our fire. He is unprotected among wolves. I fear that he can be lost to us. The whites will raise their hands against him and there will be no one to whisper into their ears that this is our Dancer."

CHAPTER NINE

Sue and Debbie were very pleased with Ramon's participation in their party clique. Grace Profitt had been so pleased that she personally gave each of the girls a $100 bill in the ladies powder room on her last night in Vegas. "I wish you had produced Ramon the first night that we met you," she had told them. "That's my only regret. He may not say much, but he makes up for it in oh so many ways." The three women laughed together at the reference.

Two days later, the two showgirls took Ramon shopping for appropriate party clothes.

"You've got to dress to impress," Debbie instructed. "We're in show business whether we are on stage or in the casino. It's our job to look glamorous."

"I like the blazer, turtleneck look," Sue added, "but we need cashmere and silk, not polyester. A couple of jackets, shirts, turtlenecks, some real quality slacks to mix and match, and some Gucci shoes."

"Socks," reminded Debbie, "and some silk bikini briefs."

"I don't know if the old dames' hearts can stand it!" Sue exploded. Often the women in the front seat of Sue's BMW talked as if Ramon was not sitting behind them.

"You know," Debbie said, "we're going to have to get cologne and handkerchiefs and everything. The poor boy has nothing."

"And a haircut," Sue said. "Let's take him to Maxine's for a makeover."

"Oh gawd, yes!" Debbie cheered. "This is so much fun. But don't let them cut his hair short."

"Of course not. He's an Indian for gawd's sake," Sue agreed. "Leave it long so he can wear it in a ponytail, but shape it, maybe a razor cut."

"Make him look like an Indian Tarzan. Remember that Greystoke Tarzan movie where he comes back to civilization and they dress him up in proper English suits? Remember that?" Debbie asked.

"He was sexy, wasn't he?" Sue smiled.

At the men's shop, Sue and Debbie made the decisions and Dancer patiently tried on what he was handed. He realized that he needed new clothes, and he was flattered by the attention the girls were giving him.

While Dancer tried on pants in the dressing room, Sue and Debbie totaled up the cash Grace Profitt had given him and added some of their own to cover the day's expenses.

"We'd better make a promise to each other

right now," Sue said seriously. "No matter how tempting it might be, neither one of us should sleep with Ramon."

"Of course," Debbie agreed, but paused. "That is, unless the other girl has a steady guy and gives her permission."

"Well, sure," Sue said. "That goes without saying."

In their main business of hustling high rollers for casino chips, Sue and Debbie recognized Ramon as a unique asset. First, he could fill out any party that included an unescorted woman. Second, his presence and his physical strength was insurance against customers who might get abusive. Third, Ramon was at the Tropicana where they could keep their eyes on him.

"He's so naive," Debbie observed.

"Yeah," Sue said. "We've got to protect him from people who might take advantage of him."

"Like those bitches Kim and Holly," Debbie reminded her. "They'll step on the train of your dress every chance they get."

"And they'll upstage you, too, with their damn big hats," Sue added.

"What would they do if they got their hands on Ramon?" Debbie speculated in horror.

"Don't even think about it! We're not going to lose Ramon after we have dressed him, manicured him, and shown him the ropes. No siree. He's our baby, and nobody else can have him."

Dancer had seldom used a mirror except for ceremonial face painting. When appearing in regalia, personal inspection by a fellow dancer sufficed. Even at the Tropicana, when he passed the huge backstage wall mirrors where three showgirls in costume could inspect themselves at once, he did not admire himself. Mirror romance was not part of his culture. But after Sue and Debbie completed their detailed makeover of his image, they made Ramon examine himself at a full-length mirror. The person he saw reflected there was a stranger to him.

Dancer was used to worn, faded, rumpled shirts and jeans. His boots, often as not worn without socks, showed the scuffs and worn-down heels of age. His only other shoes, besides his performance moccasins, were an equally worn pair of athletic sneakers that had lost their color to the dust of too many powwows. Most of Dancer's bathing over the years had been done over a bucket of cold water in a campsite or in the sinks and showers of cheap motels. When he washed his long black hair, he did it with available bar soap. Unless he was braiding his hair for a contest, he used his outstretched fingers as a wide-toothed comb to smooth the thick mass away from his face and let it dry naturally. His activity and natural oils would restore its youthful luster, but often his hair was matted and smelled pungently of sweat and cigarette smoke.

Although he had no facial hair requiring him to shave, Dancer's eyebrows were bushy and irregular. Close up, there were small irritations, even blackheads, in his complexion that were easily corrected by attention. But in the makeover process, the professionals marveled most over his perfect teeth, luxurious full-bodied hair, and classic physique. The woman who did the facial and her associate who did the manicure lingered over Dancer as if they were working on a masterpiece. From hair stylist to clothier, enthusiastic participation seemed to outweigh proprietary concern, although Sue and Debbie had a reputation as excellent tippers.

While the changes in Ramon's appearance were dramatic to the salon observers and remarkable to Sue and Debbie, they were profound to Dancer. He seemed to test facial expressions on the man in the mirror to see if the reflection was real. Then he began to laugh.

"I didn't know Indians could laugh," Debbie said through her tears.

"Ramon's no cigar store Indian anymore," Sue answered as she appraised their creation. "He is hot! Looking like that, he can go anywhere."

The girls included themselves in the reflected picture by draping their arms around Ramon and posing as if for a magazine cover.

"Is this GQ, or what?" Debbie gloated into the mirror.

"There is no going back," Sue said to Ramon. "You should look this good every day. Throw away all your old clothes, shoes, boots, everything. We're going to show you how to shampoo and condition that gorgeous mane of yours and how to take care of your face."

"Yeah," Debbie added, "remember what Billy Joel said, 'All you need is looks and a whole lot of money.'"

That night, the security guard at the Tropicana's stage door did not recognize Ramon. The cast in the rushed, crowded pre-show hallways leading from the dressing rooms to the stage froze as he passed. Nearly everyone in the show came to look and comment. Dancer had experienced the adulation of Indians on the winning of Fancy Dance competitions. He had stood in the Schemitzun National Championship spotlight and fans had thrown money at his feet for placement on the drum to honor him. He had heard large audiences applaud his dancing at the Tropicana. But the reaction of the whites to his appearance was something new, different, and especially rewarding. He felt their acceptance where he had never felt it before. It was to him as if he were being seen for the first time; seen not as an Indian, but as an equal. If wearing the rich clothes and performing the grooming rituals of the whites made him their equal, it was a thing easy enough to do.

CHAPTER TEN

Anglo hiked alone to the secret mountain cave where Nita had been honored with ritual burial, and where he had been given his Indian name and status in the Deer Clan. Although the climb from the pueblo was long and tiring, it was a place he considered refreshing.

In his pockets, Anglo carried small pouches of corn and tobacco as gifts to his spiritual mother. They would be offered at the grave, but then scattered in the wind so as not to leave signs. After the hours of silently seeking her council, he would carefully brush away evidence of his passage and tend his back trail so that even a clever explorer could not follow it. These were some of the skills he had learned from his clan brothers.

The next day, Anglo found Joseph getting water from the pueblo spring, a spigot on a piece of pipe three feet above the ground at one end of the plaza.

Each man washed his hands and cooled his face at the faucet, and then drank from the hollow of his palm. Only then did they speak.

"I am ready to go," Anglo said without looking directly into Joseph's face.

"There is a right time for every event, and there are signs to indicate every right time," Joseph responded.

"But I have no idea of what to do or what to say when I get there," Anglo admitted.

"Put aside your frightened voice and listen for the mighty Voice. It is quiet in power, strong in stillness, and Its messages are certain. Walk past the voices of the world and their meaningless persuasions. We have an ancient pledge that our function will be revealed. In every moment ask and expect an answer."

Joseph filled his bucket and beckoned Anglo to accompany him to his house. "You have not listened alone," he assured his friend. "I have been with you, and I have prepared strong medicine for your journey."

The interior of the adobe house was cool despite the heat of the morning. Anglo knew the rooms as well as he knew Nita's house, his reservation home. He stood near the center of the main room while Joseph set the water down and left his sight for a few moments. When Joseph returned, he had a small beaded pouch connected to a rawhide thong in his hand.

"Your clan and Elders have put their most precious spiritual things into this pouch. You know it as a medicine bag. We wear our medicine around our necks as an agent through which mental changes are focused into the external world. No outsider understands the purpose and the power of the medicine bag. Its contents are sacred to those who give them and to those who wear them. It is carried for both protection and healing. In times of trouble, you may secretly open your medicine bag and lay out its contents. Touch each thing. Hold it with reverence and absorb its power. Do not be surprised if the contents of the pouch seem odd.

"A bear's tooth, for example, has come from an animal who fought hand-to-claw with an ancestor, who then became a wise chief because of his scars and his victory. The tooth through the generations is our sign of bravery, that those who carry it will be brave by connection not only to the ancestor chief, but also to the bear who showed no less courage.

"Pearl has given a small polished stone that was given to Nita by her grandmother. It has been a part of our medicine for maybe 500 years. Nita would put the stone into a healing tea for a few moments before it was given to the sick. It is very strong medicine now entrusted to you."

Anglo was stunned by the significance and the sacrifice implied by the contents of the medicine bag. It was an honor that humbled him beyond any specialness that he had ever attributed to himself. The love, the complete trust, given here overflowed into his eyes.

"I know," Joseph said warmly, in recognition of the emotion. "Be at peace. You are worthy."

As the sun crossed the pueblo and began its descent into the west, Joseph explained the importance and use of each item in the medicine bag. The men sat at the cacique's table with the artifacts displayed, and Anglo took them up one by one in his hand, holding them in silence and in prayer, to accept them into his awareness, into his being.

Finally, the items were replaced into the pouch, and the opening was drawn tight and tied. Joseph then placed the leather thong around Anglo's neck and tied it into place so that the bag fit into the hollow of Anglo's chest.

"This is the heart of the people next to your heart," Joseph said.

"This is my heart," Anglo replied as he touched the bag.

"You have spoken our dreams," Joseph confirmed. "There are no words left to speak."

It was arranged that Anglo would leave for Las Vegas on the next day. Carlos was to provide the transportation in his pick-up truck. They would take two days to travel the more than 600 miles. Carlos would arrange for the first night's lodgings with his tribal cousins, the Acoma, at Sky City. The people of the white rock had occupied their 365-foot-high mesa pueblo for a thousand years. Only one Hopi pueblo could rival their claim to being the oldest continuously inhabited community in the U.S. When they arrived in Las Vegas, Carlos would remain only long enough to make the introductions between Anglo and White Wing, and to help Anglo find accommodations.

Before leaving the reservation, Anglo collected pinches of dirt from several places around the pueblo and put them into a small leather bag. He also prepared his Taos hand drum for safe transport. If the city isolated him from his people, he could always sing and drum his way back into their circle.

Anglo did not know the time of day or the calendar date when he and Carlos began their trip. He had no watch or clock, read no newspapers and watched no television. Interest in the U.S. presidency was at its peak as the summer raced towards a November election, but Anglo could not name the contestants.

Anglo measured his life by the seasons. On the road to Albuquerque, he saw the showy red prickly-pear flowers in bloom. He had eaten their sweet and gelatinous pods while working in the desert. He had eaten them raw after removing the spines, and he had eaten them roasted over a campfire. The cream-colored small massed flowers of the broad-leaved yucca were also blooming. He has tasted them in salads and as an herb in tea. He had eaten dried cakes from their banana-like fruits. He had used ropes made from their leaf fibers. He saw the piñon pines, a life

source to his people. The trees survived drought
and thrived in hard places so that their wood
could bless lodge fires in winter. And every few
seasons, the gracious piñon would give a crop of
its delicious energy-filled nuts to sustain the people. The sagebrush, the juniper, all the plants vis-
ible from the highway announced the season and
reminded Anglo that the earth was a living
being, an organism with consciousness. Respect
for these parts of the Self was no longer a feeling or an attitude; it had become a way of life
for Anglo.

And Anglo knew that among the piñon and
the mesquite were quail and roadrunner; burrowing owl and Steller's jay; golden-mantled ground
squirrel; blacktail jack-rabbit and coyote; turquoise
collared lizard; bull snake and sidewinder rattlesnake; scorpion and tarantula; tarantula hawk
wasp and brown recluse spider; tortoise laying
eggs in a burrow; and golden eagle and prairie
falcon high above. All these, too, were part of
his identity, part of Great Mother's consciousness.

Although they had only traveled 100 miles
from the reservation, Carlos took the I-40 exit to
Sky City. He very much wanted Anglo to see
the Acoma stronghold.

The road strung out across a desert plain and
there seemed no destinations ahead except the
tall mesas against the horizon. The Acoma reservation, like much of the Southwest, had once
been an ancient sea. About 270 million years ago

the sea began to dry up and become shallow. The sea bottom turned to gray limestone. Over a period of 180 million years, the sand deposited on the banks of the dying sea began to blow in the wind, forming huge sand dunes up to two miles thick. Then the dunes petrified into the hardened rock known as sandstone. On such a mesa, a high plateau with steep walls standing sentinel in a trackless desert plain, the Acomas built their fortress.

The public parking lot below the mesa was half full of tourist vehicles. Visitors paid a small fee for an uncomfortable bus ride to the pueblo, where an Acoma guide walked them around the site. An extra fee was levied for picture taking. Carlos went into the modest reception building to make arrangements for their stay in his cousin's house. Few Indians stayed overnight on the mesa except during festival events. Even the native vendors of jewelry, Kachina dolls, embroidery, and the famous thin-walled decorated pottery retired at the end of the tourist day to more modern quarters off the mesa.

"It's OK," Carlos assured Anglo back at the truck. "We'll send our backpacks up on the bus. But you and I should climb the mesa like warriors."

Until the 1940's, there had been no convenient road for getting atop Sky City. The Acomas who established the settlement had built a secret path to the top, which included stairways and foot and handholds carved into the solid rock. The concealed entry to the path required that the seeker walk to within two feet of the base at a certain point and then look right to see a narrow passage starting upward. There were many strong points en route, ladder-like climbs which afforded no cover or concealment from above, or doorways through solid rock that allowed only a single person to enter at a time. It was a design that favored the few defenders over the many attackers. Food gathering and subsistence farming was done on the valley floor below, but every person, every supply, every building material, every stick of firewood came atop the mesa via the secret path or by being hauled up on long, hand-made ropes.

Anglo had climbing experience as a result of his visits to Nita's burial cave, but the Acoma path required more care and daring.

"When I was a child," Carlos related, "our family would come for the festivals, but all us young warriors wanted to do was play on the path. You couldn't start to be a man until you made the Acoma path both up and down."

At one point, Anglo was following Carlos up a steep rockface by a series of hand and footholds. He noticed that there were several positions for holds at each level, so that people of various sizes could climb and descend safely. Suddenly, his foot slipped, but he could not fall. The deep cut and design of the handhold immediately locked his fingers at the knuckles as his body flattened against the rockface. He quickly regained the step and the handhold released him when he arched his fingers. Not only did Anglo admire the ancient Acomas, he began to climb with their confidence. When they arrived at the top of the mesa, Anglo expressed his amazement at the passage, and then asked, "Were they ever conquered?"

Carlos knew the history well. "The Spanish attacked in 1598 when the Acomas refused to give them tribute and supplies, but they were driven off. The next year, they came back in force and a great three-day battle was fought. Hundreds of Acomas were killed and the pueblo was destroyed. The Spanish took the captives to Santo Domingo for trial. Women over 12 years of age were sentenced to 25 years of hard labor. Men over 25 got the same sentence, plus having one foot chopped off. Young girls were given to the Catholic Church, and the young boys were given to the Spanish general. It is believed that the Acomas were betrayed for profit. There were good Indians and bad Indians even back then."

Carlos avoided the tourist groups and gave Anglo a tour of the pueblo. The early inhabitants had carved round catchment basins in the rock to store water from the infrequent rainfalls. It was a cleverly designed water supply. Aside from the dramatic vistas, the structure of the adobe city was familiar. The mission church was an impressive structure, but its charm was compromised by the fact that it had been built with forced Indian labor.

Their best time at Sky City was at sunset, when the tourists had departed and Carlos and Anglo were essentially alone on the silent mesa top. They ate a supper of cold fry bread and chicken cooked in peppers, given to them by Maria on their departure. There was dried fruit, too, and a jar of herbs for hot tea. They ate outdoors, sitting on the flat roof of a house with an unobstructed view of the magnificently lit sky in the west. There was a soft wind that subdued the heat of the day. It was a wordless time. And then the night came and revealed the stars. Without electric lights to steal their glory, the oval firmament was a brilliant tapestry that wrapped them in timeless awe. They could not leave it, and so they laid their blankets on the roof and slept under an infinity of ancestral eyes that watched over them and gave them peace.

CHAPTER ELEVEN

Sue was not concerned about Ramon's gambling.

"As long as we get our end," she told Debbie, "he can do what he wants with the rest. Ever since we taught him how to tip, he's become every dealer, cocktail waitress, and showroom captain's favorite Indian. They must think that he owns oil wells or something."

"He still does good with the customers," Debbie reminded. "Another couple of months and we'll start getting repeat business. You can bet old Grace Profitt will be back. Wait till she sees the improvements."

"I think it's time Ramon had his own place," Sue said. "I don't trust that Jack Menendez. He might be tempted to take Ramon freelance."

"You're right," Debbie agreed, as she filed her nails. "And gawd forbid he should get Ramon to a craps table. Let-It-Ride is bad enough, especially if you are playing with your own money."

"First rule," Sue said playfully, and they both sang in unison, "never play with your own money!"

"Ramon made a couple of grand last week, plus his Tropicana check but he was broke before the weekend. What if he can't pay his rent?" Debbie asked.

"We'll just have to take care of the details ourselves," Sue replied. "Instead of twenty percent, we'll take thirty percent and cover him on all the essentials."

"We ought to take forty and put some of it in a mutual fund for him," Debbie suggested.

"Not our problem," Sue said. "Anyway, we want him dependent on us. If he needs money, he has got to accept our dates. My biggest worry is that he finds his own girlfriend and falls in love. That would really put itchy powder in our G-strings." Both women laughed.

"If somebody has to sacrifice herself, I guess it's my duty," Debbie teased.

"No way," Sue retorted.

"Way," Debbie said with exaggeration. "I could make him fall in love with me in one night in my bedroom."

"Save it in case we need it," Sue said seriously. "And then we will cut cards for him."

The pace of Dancer's Las Vegas existence did not provide for any reflection. By the time he awoke in the late afternoon and had breakfast, it was time to do his pre-show exercise routine and head for the Tropicana, to sign-in by 7 p.m. and get into costume. Two or three times a

week, Sue and Debbie arranged dates for him
that might include a 1 a.m. supper followed by
gambling and drinking until dawn. More and
more, the women that he escorted invited him
to have sex. More often than not, he accepted.
These women were always especially generous
with their tips.

Tips, as Ramon had come to understand them,
were the primary personal expression in Las
Vegas. It was a way of saying "thanks," or "I like
you." The giving and receiving of tips signified
acceptance. It seemed akin to the concept of the
Indian Giveaway. The more you gave away, the
more honor was associated with it.

On the nights when Sue and Debbie provided
no dates, Ramon would leave the theater after
midnight to eat and gamble on his own. Actually,
he preferred to strike out alone on these nights,
visiting familiar dealers at casinos along The
Strip, and checking into lounges and restaurants
where he was now recognized. When dawn arrived, Ramon would exit The Strip by a side
street and run the mile or more back to his
apartment. No matter how much alcohol he had
had to drink, the run burned off its haze and
assured him that he would not become an alcoholic like his father.

Sleep would come to White Wing, and dreams,
but the dreams had no significance. They were
white man's dreams, dreams that required no
preparation, no purification. They were dreams

without animal spirits, without ancestral signs. They were blind, unaware dreams without wind and drum and campfire. The door to the sacred dream world, the world of connective visions, had closed. White Wing stood without voice on one side of the door, waiting for his lost brother, Ramon, to return. He could not speak. The distance had already grown too great.

CHAPTER TWELVE

If you are an Indian, the stretch of I-40 from Albuquerque, New Mexico, to the Las Vegas turn-off near Kingman, Arizona, puts you closer to more tribes and more holy places than any other highway in North America. There are Navajos, Zunis, Acomas, Lagunas, Hopis, and Apaches scattered all along the route. Detour to highways around Gallup and you could visit Canyon de Chelly, Chaco Canyon, and then, by pressing on into the southwestern corner of Colorado, you could see where the Anasazi left their legacy in the magnificent cliff dwellings of Mesa Verde. These would be holy places to you.

Further along I-40, between Gallup and Flagstaff, you could see the Petrified Forest and Meteor Crater, and then take the road beyond Flagstaff to the Grand Canyon. Your people held wonder and ceremony in these places long before white men discovered them.

A powwow Indian will remind the uninformed that his people greeted Columbus when they found him lost off the coast of America. "He thought that he was in India, so we had to be Indians." The irony has persisted.

As Anglo sped down the interstate highway and saw the road signs to Indian places, he felt a longing and a kinship to all that went unseen. He felt that he was passing through the territory of the heart. He could almost hear the drums that provide the heartbeat of the tribal nations. He wished that Carlos would get out of the traffic and find another cousin at another Sky City where they could climb like warriors to a silent place, where they could guard the ancestors twinkling in the night sky.

But the truck proceeded past Flagstaff and made the turn for Las Vegas with only minimal stops for fuel and water. There was a long stretch of Mojave Desert—dry, hot and dusty—and then suddenly a curving mountain grade onto the Hoover Dam and across into Nevada.

The high-rise hotels on the floor of the desert valley were visible from I-515 as the truck made the descent through the city of Henderson. Carlos took the Tropicana Avenue exit and began the five-mile approach to The Strip.

Nothing seemed familiar to Anglo. The city had multiplied so much since his junket days that the memory of Winn Conover could not identify any landmark other than the airport.

"Where do you want to go?" Carlos asked. "I have the directions Fox Trap gave to Ramon's apartment. It is off this street, closer in to the casinos. Maybe we could sleep there tonight."

The travel day had been nearly 10 hours in a truck without air-conditioning. Both men were parched by the summer sun. The swirling dust that came in the open windows had made a ring of grit around the necks of their T-shirts. Their western style straw hats had kept most of the dirt out of their hair. Dressed in jeans and western boots, with ponytail hair down their backs, the travelers looked more like Mexican migrant workers than Indian holy men on a mission.

Carlos found the Paradise Village address and knocked on the door for a long time before anyone answered. A bleary-eyed Jack Menendez opened the door to the extent of a security chain and stared at the odd couple on his small veranda.

"You woke me up," Jack complained. "What the hell do you want?"

"I'm Ramon's cousin," Carlos began. "This was the address—"

"He don't live here anymore," Jack spit out.

"Do you know— " Carlos began.

"No, I don't know where he lives. Maybe another unit in the complex. Check him out at the Tropicana." Jack closed the door before the final syllable.

"Let's leave the truck here," Anglo suggested, "and walk to the casino. Fox Trap said it was not far."

"Maybe we should clean ourselves up and put on a better shirt," Carlos said. "We can use the canteen in the truck and our bandannas."

When they had washed themselves at the tailgate of the truck and put on long-sleeved western-style plaid shirts, Carlos loaded their backpacks and Anglo's hand drum into the cab and covered them with a blanket. He locked the truck and the two men walked out of the apartment complex to find the Tropicana.

The hotel and casino were easily spotted as they approached The Strip intersection. A pedestrian overhead crosswalk took them from the gigantic MGM Grand complex on the north side of Tropicana Avenue to their destination on the south side of the busy city street. Once inside, the air was cool and filled with sounds of slot machines being worked. The casino itself was a maze of blinking, flashing machines separated by islands of gaming tables, and food and beverage outlets. The decor was commercial plush, with ornate carpeting and subdued lighting that gave no hint of the time of day. There were so many people moving in the aisles that Carlos and Anglo had to keep their attention on just moving from one room to another. Finally, they asked a security person for directions to the Folies showroom. The entry was up a short staircase along a colonnade fronted by retail shops. A line of people stopped them before they got to the ticket desk. Further along they could see the maitre d' station and people entering the theater. When Anglo got to the ticket desk, he learned that dinner show seating had begun. It was almost six o'clock.

"We have a few tickets left for tables in the back," the former showgirl said with a plastic smile.

Carlos whispered into Anglo's ear, "We can't afford this."

"Are you hungry?" Anglo asked. "Don't you want to see White Wing dance?"

When Carlos nodded the affirmative to both questions, Anglo removed some carefully folded bills from the front pocket of his pants and gave the ticket lady a $100 note. His change was less than $40. Carlos could not believe what his mentor had done.

"We are not dressed for this," Carlos cautioned, afraid that the tuxedoed white men at the door would not let them enter.

"Stand tall," Anglo said quietly. "We are what we are."

As Winn Conover, Anglo had seen a version of the Folies in the late 1970's in this same theater. The show had a long record of awards for best showgirls and dancers in Las Vegas. It had always played to erotic interests in its costuming, but was still considered inoffensive enough for mid-America tourists.

Not knowing what would be required, Anglo had cashed a check against his money market account before leaving Santa Fe. His divorce settlement, including a business buy-out that provided nearly $68,000 a year for ten years, was deposited to a brokerage account where the money was allocated to a portfolio of mutual funds, government bonds, and a liquid money market fund on which he could write checks. Although Anglo had anonymously contributed over $22,000 to individual needs within his pueblo, most of his settlement money was still intact due to his simple lifestyle and the personal income from working with the Silvas. Anglo, in fact, did not know the sum of his accounts. All the statements went to the brokerage firm, not the reservation. Nevertheless, when required, the prudent memory of Winn Conover knew where to go for money.

Anglo and Carlos were seated at a long banquet table set perpendicular to the stage on the back level of the showroom. Their ten dinner companions seemed to know each other, and enjoyed a lively conversation that managed to exclude the two long-haired, dark strangers at the tail end of the table. The dinner was served with efficiency by the wait staff, and the food was attractively presented on the china, but it had the flat taste of banquet fare. The reservation men ate most of their salads, twice baked potatoes, peas with tiny onions, and parfait desserts, but they had no real appetite for the prime rib.

"This ain't no free range steer," Carlos whispered. "It don't even taste real." Back on the reservation, the Silvas were accustomed to beef raised naturally by a person that they knew. Every fall they picked the animal they wanted, honored it as they would a fallen elk or mule deer, and then slaughtered it for a thanksgiving feast. Every part of the animal was used, and meat was put aside for the winter months. Commercially grown and processed beef had little relation to their experience.

As 7:30 approached, the tables were cleared of everything except wine and cocktail glasses, which generally stayed filled. Since Anglo and Carlos drank water, and then coffee after the meal, their cups were allowed to go cold. Waiters made judgments about who would leave the largest tips.

The people at their table spread and rearranged their chairs for better views of the stage. Anglo and Carlos left their seats and stood against the back wall for an unobstructed view. They had searched the program for White Wing's appearance in the show and they waited patiently through the extravaganza of costumes, loud music, a comedian and acrobats before his feature spot.

The dancers began the Native Fever tableau with feverishly wild choreographed gyrations across the expanse of the stage. The backdrop was a scene of the mountainous desert, with mock Joshua trees and artificial boulders rolled on stage to give the effect of a ceremonial plateau. The dancers were costumed in moccasins, scant loincloths with iridescent designs, and beaded headbands with single feathers. The women wore fake animal fur bound tightly across their bulging breasts. The male dancers were bare-chested. When they had completed their dance to good applause and assumed positions around the set, the showgirls began to emerge center stage through the boulders and trees. They were elaborately costumed as Indian princesses, with tall feather headpieces and ornamental feather and fringe shawl-like capes that draped from their shoulders to the floor. As they paraded to the music and extended their arms like wings to show-off the color and detail of their capes, they exposed their bare breasts. Then, as they turned, swirling the capes at the front of the stage, their tiny briefs revealed bare behinds.

Carlos, even at the back of the room, was captivated by their moves, but he was also starting to feel uneasy.

Ramon made a dramatic entrance at a crescendo in the music and dominated the center of the stage in a fury of Fancy Dancing that drew spontaneous applause.

Carlos was dumbfounded by Ramon's stage presence. He recognized the dancing, but he did not recognize the man. The regalia was all wrong. It was a shameful corruption of tradition.

And, although the dance was technically exciting, it seemed more an incredible exercise than a form of worship.

The scene ended with the dancers flanking Ramon in wild frenzy as he achieved his best moves and highest foot speed. Suddenly, the music climaxed and all the dancers on the stage froze on the last beat. The effect was not wasted on the audience, many of whom stood up and cheered. Ramon and the cast took repeated bows before the show resumed. No one noticed that the two men standing against the back wall holding their wide-brimmed, sand-colored, sweat-stained cowboy hats did not applaud. No one noticed their sadness.

CHAPTER THIRTEEN

Beauty in women has always been considered a ticket to ride elevated through a society. Beautiful women, however, will report a bumpy ride, often to unwanted destinations.

Susan Marshall was a tall, beautiful Tennessee girl, raised in Knoxville in an affluent family. Her father was a home builder. From the age of five through high school, she was one of the stars of her dancing school and a good academic student. She was voted best looking in her graduating class and began college at the University of Tennessee. At age 19, the 5-foot 10-inch freshman with a 39-23-36 figure won the title of Miss Tennessee and then competed for the Miss America title, where she placed as second runner-up.

From the time Sue was 13 years old and began to show what seemed to her an embarrassingly large bustline, boys—and all too soon men—began to pursue her. She quickly learned the carnal nature of their intentions and began to develop defenses that altered the patterns of her relationships, not only with the boys, but also with her female peers. For, although Sue originally had a sweet, outgoing nature, she restrained herself against the jealousies that her beauty seemed to attract. Sue learned to mistrust most of the overtures of friendship made to her. Men, basically, wanted to possess her. Women who considered themselves less sexually desirable betrayed themselves as bitter, and they often belittled her.

In the summer after her sophomore college year, Sue traveled to Las Vegas to visit one of her few girlfriends. She had met the girl in a beauty pageant competition. The friend was now a cocktail waitress while attempting to break into show business. During the visit, the friend encouraged Sue to accompany her to an open audition at the Tropicana, where they were seeking replacement cast members for their Folies show. In an irony that ended their friendship, Sue was asked to join the show and her friend was not.

The moment of decision for Sue was predicated on her dissatisfaction with college life, and the immaturity of its men who seemed dominated by their libidos. Her parents, of course, were shocked by her announcement, but they later came to enjoy the feeling of telling strangers that their daughter was a Folies Bergere showgirl. It seemed to them a natural, if temporary, extension of Sue's beauty pageant experiences.

For the first year, Sue was dazzled by her Las

Vegas lifestyle. She had to work hard learning the show. As the new girl, she filled in for those who had their off day. She performed in all the second line roles, perfecting the eight costume changes for each show and strengthening her neck to support the often 30-pound headpieces. She became proficient in the art of applying thick pancake makeup that made all the show-girls look so flawless in the stage lights. She learned how to keep the long, human hair eye-lashes in place and how to make a complete cos-tume change in less than one minute. And, finally, Sue learned how to use her beauty to make real money.

Debbie Harris, an inch taller and an inch big-ger at the waist than Sue, had the same trouble with men that Sue had experienced, but she faired better with her female peers because she did not challenge them intellectually. Debbie was a cheerleader in high school who sometimes struggled to keep up her grades. She almost mar-ried the star of the football team, but when he went away to college and she didn't, the prom-ises that had been made in exchange for pas-sionate sex evaporated. Debbie found herself teaching at the same dancing school where she had taken every class over the preceding 12 years. It was a subsistence life that only added to the pressure of older men who wanted to use her.

Having been told all her life how beautiful and talented she was, Debbie left her home in

Raleigh, North Carolina and went to Los Angeles to get into the movies. Her naivete was rapidly stripped away in casting waiting rooms full of girls like her. She waited tables, considered topless dancing, and dated the wrong men for the wrong reasons. When a date took her to Las Vegas and turned drunk and abusive, she abandoned him and decided to stay in Las Vegas, where jobs were easier to find and where there were still opportunities to get into show business.

Debbie was hired at the same time that Sue joined the Folies cast. As the two new showgirls, they looked to each other immediately for support and soon agreed to share an apartment together.

During their initial year at the Tropicana, Sue and Debbie could not keep their income. In an extravagant town, they practiced extravagance in most of the ways that tourists do, including gambling. Their status as showgirls provided them with multiple date offers. Notes were passed backstage between shows proposing everything from midnight suppers to marriage. The girls learned to be selective, depending on cues from the casino staff for introductions to men. They learned early to stay away from the Vegas working class as men who could only aspire to use them. In that year, Sue and Debbie still saw the Folies as only the first step in their show business careers. Dates were to be considered as upwardly mobile career contacts. The men that they wanted to meet were entertainment vice presidents, Hollywood agents, film producers and directors. But what they got were doctors, lawyers, and business executives out for a fantasy experience. Some were rich and polished, with education and manners. Others were rich and crude to the point of being obnoxious. What they all had in common was the desire to have beautiful showgirls on their arms, to parade at the casino tables as evidence of their virility and power. And then, of course, there was the hope that their lust would be fulfilled. And if not, there would always be the consolation that all who saw them together would assume it so.

The girls knew what lust was. It was cleavage and perfume, and putting your head on a man's shoulder and whispering anything into his ear. It was the illusion of public intimacy that was their stock in trade. And if a date was generous with his gambling chips, almost any personality and appearance flaws could be endured without the loss of professional smiles. But if the money did not flow, the girls excused themselves early or disappeared after a visit to the powder room.

Sue and Debbie made a pact. Neither one wanted to marry a rich, middle-aged customer or a Las Vegas hustler. They never wanted to depend on any man for their security. They were nineties women. They realized that there was a

time limit on their beauty and on their stamina
for working two jobs. They planned to work into
their mid-thirties and then retire from show business on their investments. They were not going
to invest in sleaze operations, or allow drugs and
alcohol to bring them down into working in strip
joints. They were not prostitutes.

By the time Ramon came into their lives, Sue
and Debbie each owned a fashionable house and
an impressive car. Each had an investment portfolio. But the real investments could not be acknowledged. Each income tax statement reported
a gross income of $33,800 from their Tropicana
employment. What went unreported was an average of $125,000 a year each girl made from si-
phoning off casino chips while accepting
generous gratuities from her escorts. Much of the
cash went under the table to businesses in need
of silent partners. Sue and Debbie owned pieces
of legitimate businesses like beauty parlors, coin
laundries, and apartment buildings all over Las
Vegas.

"What are we going to do about having kids?"
Debbie asked Sue, the leader of their clique.

"Vegas is not a town for raising kids. I don't
care what the promotions say," Sue answered.
"Let's buy a place in Northern California or
somewhere that's cool in the summer. Let's put
down some roots and scout out the marriage
prospects. There have got to be some good men
left who don't need to come to Las Vegas. Let's

find two of these guys, when it is time, and give them some babies."

Sue was a blond. Debbie was a brunette. Both girls wore their hair cropped stylishly short in order to accommodate the wigs that they wore in the show and on dates.

"And then we can let our hair grow out," Debbie said wistfully.

"Yes," Sue agreed. "Then we can be ourselves again."

CHAPTER FOURTEEN

At the end of the show, the dinner crowd left the room and the service staff began a hurried re-set for the cocktail show. Anglo asked a busboy for directions backstage, and was pointed to a door at the side of the theatre which opened into a wide catering access hallway. The cast door was at the end of the hall. A security guard would not let Anglo and Carlos enter, but he agreed to get a message to Ramon that he had a cousin waiting at the stage door.

With only an hour between shows, most cast members waited in one of the 18 dressing rooms backstage. They talked from stools set before long makeup tables lined with mirrors, or read magazines or books. In the hallways, small groups of cast members visited, everyone still in makeup. Ramon was standing with Debbie talking about their plans for the night. Sue had ducked out to a casino lounge to meet their dates and make arrangements for after the late show. A stagehand gave Ramon his message. "One of your cousins is asking for you at the casino door."

Ramon could not guess who it might be. There were a hundred powwow friends who might claim to be his cousin. Perhaps it was Fox Trap stopping over between powwows. Fox Trap would not have his new address and he would no longer be a compatible visitor. Too much had changed since any Indian with a blanket could sleep on Dancer's floor.

The guard opened the double fire doors to the catering hallway and Ramon was suddenly confronted with Carlos, his blood cousin from the reservation, and an older stranger. The two cousins greeted each other warmly with a hug.

"What are you doing here?" Ramon asked. "Is my mother okay?"

"She is fine," Carlos reassured. "Still the best cook in the pueblo."

Carlos turned to Anglo and made the introduction. He used his tribal name.

Ramon extended his hand. "So you are Anglo. I heard the stories, but I thought it was just another tribal myth." The handshake lingered as if each man were trying to learn something about the other. There was prolonged eye contact for the same purpose. "What brings you so far from Santa Fe?"

"We came to see you," Carlos interjected, "but you moved, and we had to come here."

"You want to see the show?" Ramon offered.

"We saw the show just now," Carlos said flatly.

"I could have gotten you a discount or maybe a couple of comps if you had asked me."

"No problem," Carlos said. "I was wondering, can we stay with you tonight? We've been on the road all day."

"Sure," Ramon said. "I'll get you the keys and the address. It's in the same complex, Paradise Village."

"We know," Carlos said without satire.

"I can't see you after the show because I have some business, but you can use the place and I will see you in the morning, early. We can talk for a while and then I have to sleep. Sleep days, work nights. That's what we have to do in show business."

"We understand," Anglo said as his first words. "We are grateful for your hospitality."

Ramon got the keys from his dressing room and sent the men off to rest. He thought it odd that the anglo should accompany Carlos, but questions were impolite. If the stories were true, Anglo was to be given the respect of a tribal Elder.

"Who was it?" Debbie asked when they resumed their conversation.

"It was really a cousin, Carlos, from my home reservation. He brought another man who has been adopted into our clan. I guess you would say that he is my uncle."

"Why are they here?" Debbie asked with purpose.

"Just visiting," Ramon responded. "They were even paying customers for the last show."

Back at Ramon's small apartment, the two visitors pulled out the queen-sized sofa bed in the living area. The efficiency kitchen was separated from their area by a wet bar. Ramon's bedroom was respected, except as a passthrough to the bathroom. The two men removed their boots and pants and stretched out on the bed. The air-conditioning had the room so cold that they had to cover themselves with their blankets.

After a long silence, Carlos asked, "What do you think?"

"I try not to think," Anglo answered. "The appearance seems to be that our brother has dropped his eagle feather and that he dances on in ignorance of his loss and of his humiliation."

"This is a white man's apartment," Carlos observed. "I see nothing that ties White Wing to our people."

"It probably came furnished," Anglo said to comfort. "It is better to seek signs than to make judgements where they are absent."

Carlos could not rid himself of the image of Ramon performing on the Tropicana stage. He considered the act to be sacrilege.

"How can White Wing throw off a whole life of honoring our traditions in a few months?" Carlos asked with emotion.

"The path of discipline and devotion is steep and hard to climb, but the path of pleasure is all downhill. The steps quicken, and then the feet break into an uncontrolled run toward the bottom. Even a strong will loses its intent to the body."

"You answer like Joseph," Carlos said with respect.

Anglo laughed. "Don't honor me too much. I was just thinking that I wished he were here instead of me."

Although it was well after 10 p.m. and the two men on the bed had been active since dawn, they could not sleep. "Let's sing," Anglo said after a half hour of silence.

"The neighbors will attack us," Carlos said with humor.

"They sleep days," Anglo replied, sitting up on the edge of the bed. "With the air-conditioning running so high, they might feel us, but they won't hear us."

"Let's eat the rest of Maria's fry bread and chicken," Carlos suggested. "And let's light some sweetgrass and purify this place."

Anglo and Carlos folded the bed back into place and assembled the hand drum, rattles and sweetgrass for the purification ritual. Carlos danced the burning sweetgrass from room to room while Anglo beat the drum and sang a purification song. And then the alarms in the room smoke detectors went off. Not knowing the source of the loud piercing sounds, Carlos assumed the defensive crouch of a frightened animal. Anglo set the drum aside and silenced the two alarms by removing their batteries. A bewildered Carlos got to his feet, and encouraged by the resumption of the drum, completed the ritual. Only then did the two men enjoy a mutual chuckling that grew into unabashed laughter.

"Was that a sign, Uncle?" Carlos managed.

"A very loud one," Anglo heartily agreed.

They decided to eat next and sat on high stools at the wet bar to share the remains of Maria's food. Then they spread their blankets on the floor and sat across from each other to sing, as they had so many nights before. Anglo beat the sometimes complex rhythms on the Taos drum and took the role of head singer by selecting the songs and their durations. Carlos, who had taught Anglo most of the tribal songs that his adopted uncle knew, could not have been more pleased. Anglo was worthy as a head singer, and Carlos had helped him become so.

The Indians sang past midnight, and then calm, untroubled, and refreshed, they pulled out the bed and were peacefully asleep within a few minutes.

Ramon and the showgirls had just arrived backstage after the finale, and were changing both costumes and makeup for the business ahead. The party of six would end up at dawn downtown at the Golden Nugget. The customers would attempt to get the showpeople up to their suites, but the advances would be professionally deterred. Sue and Debbie shared a cab and offered to drop Ramon at Paradise Village, but he chose instead to walk back to The Strip and then to run the rest of the way home.

"I run every night," he told them. "I'm almost sober by the time I get home. Then I can sleep without the bed starting to whirl."

Anglo and Carlos were up before dawn. They made herbal tea and ate some dried fruit for energy. Then they went to greet the day on Ramon's front door veranda. Sitting on their folded blankets on the concrete slab, flanked by ornamental cactus, their backs against the wall, they would not have been noticed by passersby in the early morning shadows. They waited in silence for Mother Earth and Father Sky to be reunited by the sun. In this way each dawn was anticipated as a blessing rather than a herald of toil.

When Dancer arrived in full stride at the apartment door, the sky had lightened, but the shadows still concealed his visitors. He was startled when he finally saw them.

"Ya hey!" Ramon said in reflex.

"Ya hey," the two shadows replied.

"We were about to light the pipe," Anglo advised him. "Will you smoke with us?"

Dancer removed his summer-weight silk sports jacket and joined his kin on the blanket. Anglo lit the short, elbow-shaped ceremonial pipe, smoked, and passed it to Dancer, who in turn smoked and passed the pipe to Carlos. The pipe went around the intimate circle several times before Anglo spoke.

"I have brought you a gift," he said, as he produced a small leather pouch which hung by a thong at his belt and handed it to Dancer.

Dancer untied the thong which secured the bag and then held it closer to his face so that he could view its contents. It appeared to be dirt mixed with small pebbles, trace pieces of straw and splinters of firewood.

Anglo explained, "This is earth collected in the four directions from the plaza of our tribal pueblo. It is now mixed with earth from the highest point of the mesa where the Acoma built their Sky City. May you always have your people's ground to dance on."

"How do you know to do these things?" Dancer asked in amazement.

"Like our ancestors, I sweat, I listen, I dream," Anglo answered.

"You say 'like our ancestors,' but you are a white man," Ramon said with a hint of challenge.

"When the white churches took the Indian children away from their families and their traditions, they said that the children would become like apples, red on the outside but through and through white on the inside. I say to you that I am a melon, white on the outside and red through and through on the inside."

Carlos liked the analogy. "It's true," he said to Ramon. "Anglo sits with the Elders in council and in the Kachina ceremonies. He sings our songs. He beats our drum."

Ramon did not want to hear what Carlos was saying. He was rigid in his distrust of whites. He responded to Carlos as if Anglo were a distant third person.

"I suppose that he can dance our dances then."

Carlos sensed the edge on Dancer's response and let the disrespect evaporate before he answered. "Anglo Straight Dances like the Elder that he is. To dance in his footprints is an honor."

Anglo took the opportunity to extend the pipe once more to Dancer, but he held up his palm and then got to his feet.

"It is then with respect," Dancer said with forced formality, "that I leave you and go to my bed. I can be a better host this afternoon when I am rested." Then he went inside. The door opened and Anglo and Carlos felt the rush of cold refrigerated air as it closed.

CHAPTER FIFTEEN

"Now what do we do?" Carlos asked. "It's dawn, and we can't talk to Ramon again until this afternoon."

"Let's get out of the city," Anglo suggested. "Joseph told me about a holy place called Valley of Fire. Let's go there."

"Yes, yes," Carlos said. "Let's go early, before the temperature hits 105 degrees. I'll fill the canteen. We can get a map and directions at a gas station."

The trip north via I-15 took the two men past Nellis Air Force Base into a broad Mojave Desert valley rimmed by gray limestone mountains. It took less than an hour to reach the exit to Valley of Fire State Park. A Southern Paiute store at the southern edge of their Moapa River Reservation was the first oasis that they had seen for miles, so they stopped. It was still very early, and few tourists were expected to brave the summer heat for the sake of a geological wonder, so there was no one in the store except its manager and a single employee.

The store was an assemblage of prefabricated, trailer-shaped buildings bound together and air-conditioned for the tourist trade. It contained rows of slot machines; tables and racks of fireworks; long upright coolers filled with beer, bottled water, and sodas; a clothing section featuring T-shirts; a snack food department and even a corner devoted to serious books on Native American subjects.

Anglo looked at the books while Carlos scanned for something to eat. He ended up buying cold bottled water, sticks of a locally produced beef jerky, and some fried fruit turnovers. Anglo added two books to the items at the register and paid.

The road to the west entrance of the park was long and dusty. Their own desert around the Rio Grande Valley seemed lush by comparison. They could smell the pungent odor of the creosote bushes, and then ahead they began to see the red rocks.

The same sea that once flooded the southwest and then dried up to leave gigantic sand dunes, which petrified to create the mesa for Sky City, also covered the Valley of Fire. But in this special place, sand and mud plastered over the ancient limestone seabed which had erupted into mountains by the colliding of gigantic continental plates. Exposure of the deep sediments to air caused many of the iron compounds within the sand and mud to oxidize and form rust, which petrified over time. The resulting tilted sandstone plates are now red and purple, lavender and pink. The layers and folds stand out in sharp relief, as rain and wind have eroded pockets, caves, and odd-shaped windows on the sky into their formations. Here the supreme sculptor and painter combined to render works in spectacular form and brilliant color. The site is a dry desert valley with gray mountains as a backdrop. Once it was wetter and cooler and alive with bighorn sheep. The first human beings who found it must have been awed.

There was no Park Ranger at the gate, but there were envelopes and instructions for depositing the entrance fee in a slotted box. Anglo had purchased a large-format pictorial guidebook to the park at the Paiute store, so they decided to explore the area without a stop at the Visitor Center.

They saw the first petroglyphs at Atlatl Rock, a maze of formations which also included petrified logs. The clear shape of an atlatl, a notched stick used to increase the accuracy and distance of a thrown spear, had been pecked into a face of Aztec sandstone. The surface for the artwork was a black patch of desert varnish, a veneer caused by evaporating water that left behind a residue of iron and manganese over a period of thousands of years. Anglo read from the guidebook. The petroglyphs were created by Pueblo Indian ancestors, the Anasazi, the ancient ones. On some rockfaces where there was desert varnish, a carver would have spent hours with a sharp handstone to accomplish his task. The work included ritual signs, maps, historical records, animal images—especially bighorn sheep—and suspected clan and personal marks. The relevance of the signs for the Valley of Fire inhabitants had begun perhaps 3,000 years ago and ended in 1150 A.D., when the Anasazi departed the area.

When the men came back to the parking area, the sun was up enough to require sunglasses, but they still encountered no other people. Near the center of the park they turned onto the Visitor Center road, but then turned again before the parking lot onto a road which climbed a narrow, high-walled gorge to the trailhead entrance to Petroglyph Canyon and Mouse's Tank. There were no vehicles at the trailhead parking area, just a bathroom shelter and a posted trail map.

"We'd better carry the canteen," Carlos said.

The trail began in deep, powdery, pink-red sand.

"Let's go barefoot while we can," Carlos suggested, and the two men took off their boots and socks. The sand was dry and warm, and the fine granules quickly coated their feet.

The passage through the gorge narrowed—with rockfaces towering 40 feet above them—and then opened into clearings dotted with boulders, pale green stunted sagebrush, waxy-leafed creosote bushes, and isolated clumps of dried yellow grasses. Carlos warned Anglo not to step on a tiny desert cholla cactus whose thorn was painful. There were streaks in the sand where a lizard had passed, and high above in a cloudless deep blue sky a turkey vulture soared on five-foot wings. Their presence was announced by the shrill warning of a canyon wren.

The walls of the canyon were full of niches and holes large enough for one or two men to find shelter and sleep. A mesquite tree grew precariously on a steep wall, and hardy lichen covered the north faces of granite boulders which lay on the canyon floor.

The petroglyphs were abundant. Originally they had been carved at eye level, but water had so eroded the canyon bed that now the artwork was displayed 20 feet above their heads in some places.

"The Paiutes call this valley the Place of Birth," Carlos said. "They say that some of the old shamen of the Nuwuvi can read the petroglyphs, but they don't tell what they mean to any college professors."

About a quarter of a mile into the canyon there was a fork. The right fork led quickly into a dead end blocked by a massive boulder. The left fork opened into a sandy clearing about 20 feet across, with a sheer rockface towering above on the right. There were no carved signs to mark the place. To the left, scattered boulders channeled the canyon into a steep narrow slit with no outlet. Straight ahead, two tall rockfaces came together into a V-shape which closed the canyon. The small box canyon that ended here resembled hundreds like it in the valley. There seemed nothing unusual about the place. What could not be seen, however, was that a third large boulder was positioned below the conjunction of the V-shaped formation. Being posed vertically against the rock walls, it created a deep natural stone pocket, a tank. When summer thunderstorms swept the desert, the rockfaces and the box canyon floor funneled torrents of rain into the basin.

Mouse's Tank had a 3 x 7 foot mouth and was 11 feet deep. A second, concealed oblong hole, 5 x 6 feet, was 12 feet deep. Indians who knew this secret could exist here, while others had to leave or die of thirst.

In the mid 1890's, a Paiute Indian named Mouse eluded the capture of a white posse by hiding in the labyrinth of canyons in the Valley of Fire. The fragmented history of whites reports Mouse as an outlaw. The Indians, whose homelands along the Muddy River were usurped by Mormons, remember that Mouse stole a knife, and then was hunted down and killed by the Mormon sheriff for stealing a tomato from the garden of an Indian woman.

Anglo had to brace himself so that he could lean between the boulders to see the water five feet below the clearing floor. There were dead insects floating on the surface and the water was probably warm—perhaps even putrid from animals who had fallen into the tank—but it was still the stuff of life.

Carlos looked into the tank and then said, "You need a gourd to lower on a string. It ain't no place to take a swim."

The light spearing onto the canyon floor was becoming molten. Anglo and Carlos replaced their boots and retreated to a wide indentation in a wall where the canyon was narrow and cool. They sat in the shadow of the rockface and drank from the canteen.

"Somebody told me that whites need five times as much water as Indians under the same sun. We are supposed to have very tight pores. But even I don't want to be in this canyon when it gets to be 125 degrees."

"Let's stay a while longer and listen," Anglo said.

As the sun achieved its apex in the cloudless desert sky, even the snakes and lizards ceased movement. The canyon was silent. The two visitors became reverent supplicants. And because the canyon passage provided few shaded niches, they sat where the petrogyph makers had sat under the same sun. They sat, like them, in the oven of creation, waiting for understanding.

"It is simple, isn't it?" Anglo finally said to break the silence. "God is life, life itself. All the theologies and myths are desperate metaphors of this Reality. There is nothing we have to know. There is nothing we have to do. The awe we feel sitting in this quiet place is the awareness of those who sat here before us. We are part of them and the red sandstone and the call of the canyon wren. All of this and every interconnected form is sacred."

"Yes," Carlos said. "Those are good words for what is in my heart. Our ancient brothers hear us and they are happy. Today they carved the story of a good hunt on the canyon wall. Today they made signs to show us the way to water. Today we join them in the shade of this wall. Thousands of years are joined in this moment. I am smiling. You are smiling. They are smiling. We are together."

"Such words from a man who collects firewood," Anglo said with pride. "How could you not also be a tribal priest?"

"I am a priest only because I walk your path."

"And I am on the path only because I see with your eyes."

"Joseph says that you speak his dreams. Now I understand," Carlos said.

"Let us now bring our son and brother, White Wing, into our circle. I have brought blue corn and tobacco to leave for our ancestors. I seek their help in this mission."

Carlos made a sign with his hands that gave a sacred affirmation to what Anglo had said, and then the ritual offering began.

No one disturbed them. And when they were done, they hiked out of the canyon to the truck and drove back to Las Vegas.

CHAPTER SIXTEEN

Dancer awoke in his curtained dark bedroom. He slept naked under a sheet and a blanket, so he put on a robe against the air-conditioning chill when he got up. Not finding his visitors in the apartment, he opened the front door to see if Carlos's truck was in the parking space. He found the visitors sitting on their blankets in the shade of the veranda wall. The afternoon light was white in its brightness and the dry heat was extreme. As far as Dancer knew, Carlos and Anglo had been sitting on the veranda since he had left them that morning.

"Ya hey," Ramon greeted them. "Come into the cool. I got to take a shower, and then we can get something to eat. I know a good place."

The Frontier had a large free parking lot, so Carlos parked his truck easily and the two visitors followed their host into the casino, past the clatter and ringing of the slot machines, to Margarita's Cantina. Ramon was greeted by several of the Mexican wait staff as he was led to a booth.

The feast of fajita wings, pollo pepita, rice and beans was satisfying, and Ramon was obviously enjoying the celebrity that his previous patronage and tips had earned. He urged his guests to try the margaritas or at least a Carta Blanca Beer, but they accepted only water. Twice during the meal, Ramon left the table to talk and laugh with the restaurant captain and with one of the cooks behind the high counter of the open kitchen. Even at three in the afternoon, the place was festive and busy.

Anglo said little more than was required to order his meal. Carlos and Ramon conversed in a mix of their three languages about mutual friends from the reservations around Santa Fe. Carlos obliged with the news from home, while Ramon seemed easily distracted. Their talk was erratic and awkward.

In the Indian world, a host never turns away a guest, especially a clan member, and he never asks how long the guest will stay. Carlos was surprised when Ramon asked the impolite question.

"I must leave soon," Carlos said with a glance to Anglo. "My father needs my help in our firewood business." He paused, not sure of the effect of his next words. "Anglo will be staying."

Ramon's face returned to the neutral pose that so confounded whites because it betrayed no emotion. It was the native face, carved into wood and stone, that seemed to them so stoical, even inscrutable. For Indians, the face was a cultural mask behind which a person could wait for the signs and portents of right action. The drumbeat creates harmony by synchronizing each step. It is a metaphor for being in step with Nature, with the Great Spirit. Indian faces wait for the beat that signals the time for responding.

"Will you stay with me?" Ramon asked Anglo. The words were more a question than an invitation.

"I will stay," Anglo said simply. "It would be a great honor to dance with the head dancer of our tribe."

Ramon excused himself as soon as they returned to the apartment. He did not want an adopted uncle, a pretend Indian, dropped into his life no matter what the stories implied. But what could he do? His blood cousin had delivered the man and shown him the respect due an Elder. They had smoked together, and he had accepted the gift of sacred ground. How did the anglo know to give such a gift? It was very confusing. He needed to talk to Sue and Debbie, his best friends in Vegas. Perhaps they could tell him what to do.

"Let me get this straight," Sue said after Ramon had spoken. "You have to take this complete stranger into your apartment as a point of tribal honor although this old guy is not even a real Indian?"

"Yes," Ramon confirmed. "But he is adopted. He has a tribal name. He is considered a holy man to my people."

"I'm Catholic," Debbie injected, "but that don't mean I have to provide room and board to any priest or nun who shows up on my doorstep."

"I cannot turn him away," Ramon lamented.

"Then, ignore him," Sue said. "You are only at your pad to sleep and clean up anyway. So tell him that you are sorry, but you can't entertain him. You will hardly see each other."

"Don't leave any food around," Debbie said. "Empty the fridge."

"Good idea," Sue agreed. "With no food and no company, the guy will get bored and go home. Just totally ignore him with a bunch of excuses, and he'll go away."

"You can stay over at my house a couple of days," Debbie offered. "He'll get the message. I bet you a five stack of red chips that he doesn't last a week."

After the last show, Ramon went out with the girls although they did not have customer dates. They took him to their hide-a-way lounge, a quiet bar in the suburbs that stayed open until dawn for the Vegas late shift. It was a place where performers, managers and dealers could relax away from their casino working environment. There was not a single slot machine in the place.

By the time Ramon got home, Carlos was loading his truck.

"It's a long drive," Carlos said. "I'll come back for Anglo when it is time. Anglo is a wise man. It would be good for you to talk with him."

Carlos could say no more. It was not his place to say more. He could not remain although it gripped his heart to go. Warriors had to fix their faces and do their duty. This was his duty. Anglo had an even harder duty. His victory was not assured.

Carlos held Anglo's hand in a tight grip and put his other hand on his uncle's forearm to pour into him all the strength of his youth. They parted without words because they saw into each other's hearts.

Ramon waved from the veranda as Carlos pulled away in his truck, and then he left Anglo standing on the walkway as he entered the apartment. As he got into bed in the chilly room with the closed door, Ramon did not think about what Anglo might do that day. He only thought what a long ride Carlos would have when he soon returned to pick up the pretend-Indian Uncle.

CHAPTER SEVENTEEN

In the afternoon when Ramon began his day, he found Anglo sitting in the outside heat of the veranda. He explained that he had dry cleaning to fetch, an appointment with his hair stylist to keep, and other errands that would occupy the hours before showtime. He warned Anglo that a housekeeper would come to clean the apartment and change the bed.

The housekeeper worked for Sue and Debbie, and in addition to her chores, she reported on Ramon's personal habits. She was instructed to look for signs of female guests and to keep Ramon supplied with the shampoo, conditioner, facial treatment and colognes that they required for his beauty regimen.

Dancer gave Anglo no opportunity for conversation. At dawn, Anglo waited for his arrival on the veranda, but Ramon would not be deterred from sleep. On awaking in the mid-afternoon, he spent an hour in the bathroom and then hurried out with as few words as possible.

For the first three days Anglo stayed near the

apartment, subsisting on food he purchased at a grocery store near UNLV. Then he began to keep Dancer's hours. If Ramon wanted to run like a deer and be elusive in the tangled forest of casinos, then Anglo would have to become a tracker. The good hunter knows the detailed habits of the animal that he seeks. He follows. He observes. He waits patiently for his opportunity.

Anglo gained access to the back areas of the Tropicana at its loading docks. In Virginia Beach, he had worked the loading dock of a grocery store while attempting closure with his wife and children, so he knew food handling and inventory control. When he offered to help truck drivers unload, and performed in an efficient manner, no one questioned his presence. Within a few nights he had carried goods to various areas in the house kitchen, and was even being greeted by regular employees. His willingness to help wherever needed earned him a staff apron, and even an occasional tip from employees who could take an extra break while the Indian named Booker did their work. Seeing him night after night, the security staff not only accepted his presence, but appreciated his constant willingness to fetch coffee and pastries from the employee canteen.

The guards at the casino-side Tiffany Theatre stage door, where the performers came and went, began to rely on Booker's nightly runs. They told him about their personal lives, about their problems on the job, and he listened carefully and intently.

"That guy Booker is all right," one guard told his relief. "You ought to talk to him sometime when he brings the donuts. The dude don't say much, but what he says is deep, partner, deep."

"I know the man," the other mildly protested. "Most polite kitchen helper I ever knew. And the most unusual. I called him a brother last night, and he lit up like our 13,000-bulb show curtain. I mean, you say something nice to the man and he looks at you like you gave him a jackpot."

Anglo did not ingratiate himself with the security guards by design or to gain an advantage. The fact that he had worked his way from the loading dock to the Folies Bergere stage door was the path dictated by his need to observe Dancer. That he left his generous character along the route was merely the sign of his passage. Nothing was disturbed. It was the way a true Indian walks through a woods or across a desert valley.

And like a good scout on a trail, Anglo was invisible to what he observed. Ramon and the two girls exited the stage door about 20 minutes after the late show finale, and walked past the service staff in the catering hallway without noticing Anglo in his apron and Tropicana baseball cap. He was unseen because he blended into the environment. In the casino, as Ramon and the girls acted out the extravagance fantasy for their customers, Anglo watched the elegant party at the baccarat table from a forest of slot machines, indistinguishable from the common player. And when they moved from table to bar to restaurant, and even to another casino, Anglo followed them without being seen.

At the end of the night, Anglo sometimes saw Ramon accept his customer's advances and go to her room. On nights when Ramon gambled and drank alone, except for the fellow night travelers around him, Anglo kept pace and watched. Soon he came to anticipate the end of Ramon's nightly run and was able to precede him to the apartment, and be waiting on the blanket near the front door when Ramon arrived. Ramon assumed that the pretend Indian holy man was there for his sunrise ritual.

"You owe me," Sue demanded of Debbie. "You bet the uncle would be gone in a week, and he's still here two weeks later."

"What does he do all day?" Debbie asked in frustration. "Every time Ramon sees him he is just sitting on a blanket at his doorstep. Is this getting spooky, or what? Does he sleep? Does he eat?"

"Angelina says that she changes the sheets on the sofa bed and that there is strange food in the fridge, so he must sleep and eat sometime."

"You ever notice how Ramon gets a funny expression on his face sometimes when we are out?" Debbie asked reflectively. "He looks up suddenly like somebody hit him with a spitball, and he doesn't know where it came from. You ever notice that lately?"

"I know what you are saying," Sue concurred. "Maybe it is some Indian thing."

"Yeah, or maybe it's the way we feel when somebody is staring at us," Debbie said.

"People are always staring at us," Sue laughed.

"You know what I mean," Debbie protested.

"Maybe the old uncle is watching Ramon," Sue speculated. "Why else is he hanging around?"

"Let's see what the old guy does on our next day off," Debbie proposed.

"Oh, come on Honey, we've got better things to do on our only day off than spy on some pretend Indian."

"Like what?" Debbie challenged. "It might be fun."

"Or it might be hot and boring," Sue countered.

A few days later, Sue and Debbie watched Ramon's apartment from the confines of Sue's BMW. They debated about a discreet distance and about running the motor for the air-conditioning, and compromised by using binoculars and leaving the car running. It was dark when they took up their position. Near dawn a cab stopped at the apartment, and they were surprised to see the uncle emerge.

"It's him for sure," Sue advised. "He's wearing a baseball cap and has a ponytail." She paused. "He went in, and now he is back on the porch with his blanket. He is sitting down. Ah ha! And Ramon thinks that he just got up."

The girls waited, crouched in the car, taking turns with the binoculars until Ramon surprised them by running through the pools of light from the streetlights up to the apartment.

"He's stopping to say something to the uncle, and now he is going in," Debbie reported.

The sky grew lighter and the girls saw the uncle go into the apartment. They waited as full light emerged and the car engine began to sputter from its hours of idling. Sue turned off the AC and put the electric windows down.

"We could be off to Lake Tahoe playing Thelma and Louise, but no, you had to do the Cagney and Lacey thing instead," Sue complained. "Uncle what's-his-name has gone to bed. We can't sit here all day."

"We're on a stake-out," Debbie admonished. "I'll take the first shift and keep you advised on the car cellular. You can take a cab home. Come back in four hours."

"And what are you going to do about food and water?" Sue asked pointedly.

"I'll use the phone and have somebody deliver," Debbie said.

"To a parked car?"

"Why not?" Debbie insisted. "But first I want to call AAA for gas and a battery charge. I want the AC back on."

Debbie's shift was unproductive, but she kept

busy on the phone, having the car serviced in place and frozen daiquiris delivered every hour. Sue arrived by cab about 10:30 with a deli lunch and a cooler full of iced tea. When she got into the car she saw the daiquiri cups.

"Have you been drinking on duty?"

"Fire me," Debbie pleaded. "Nothing has happened. Nobody has left the apartment."

"I told you the uncle went to bed," Sue said.

"Sure, we know that now," Debbie shot back. "I need a shower. I think I am starting to stink, and I have got to pee so bad you don't want to know."

"Get out of here," Sue instructed, "but stay by the phone in case the uncle goes out."

Sue fought boredom and the inquisitive looks of passersby for four hours until Debbie returned.

"Anything?"

"Nothing."

"What do you want to do?" Debbie asked.

"I want to pull your hair out by the roots," Sue said with a scowl, "but if he is going to move, it's going to be soon, so let's wait."

Ramon was the first to exit the apartment in the mid-afternoon. His taxi took him away from their position. A few minutes later, the uncle emerged and began walking toward Tropicana Avenue.

"The game is afoot," Sue said.

"Who said that?" Debbie asked.

"Sherlock Holmes, you dummy."

"I knew that," Debbie shot back. "It was a test, and you passed."

"You passed gas," Sue teased.

The girls were surprised when the uncle went directly to the loading docks of their casino and went inside. They quickly parked the car and followed him into the maze of storage rooms, walk-in freezers and cold boxes necessary for the hotel's food and beverage service.

They were stopped in a broad serviceway by a forklift driver, "Hey ladies, you lost?"

Sue showed her employee badge and explained that they were looking for a man who had just come into the building. "He dropped his watch in the parking lot," she lied.

"Ask the dock foreman," he advised them.

At the foreman's receiving desk, Sue described the uncle and told her lost watch lie.

"You must be talking about Booker," he told them. "He's a truck driver's helper. If he's here, he is probably moving goods into the kitchen or storage areas."

At the office of one of the huge production kitchens, they were told that Booker was a swing shift worker. "I think he fills in wherever he is needed. Try the catering station upstairs. They might know where he is working today."

"What's going on?" Debbie asked. "Is he really working here?"

The girls went carefully from one back-of-the-house area to another, expecting to encounter the subject named Booker at any turn. Surprisingly, although they were dressed casually, no one asked for their IDs. Finally they saw someone whom they recognized, a woman in the banquet department who had waited on them many times. When they asked about Booker, the middle-aged black woman smiled broadly.

"Oh yeah, we know Booker-man, Honey. He's our swing man. You know, fills in here and there whenever we need help. We love Booker. Don't know how we ever got along without him."

Finally they reached familiar territory, the service hallway for catering the Folies dinner show, and talked to the security guard at the stage door.

"I know Booker," the familiar guard said. "Fine fellow, Miss Sue. Salt of the earth. Do anything for you."

"Is he an employee?" Debbie asked.

"Well, sure, I assume he is an employee."

"Have you ever seen his ID badge?" Sue asked.

"Actually, no. I suppose he clips it on his pocket and the pocket gets covered by the work apron. Is there any problem?"

"No," Sue responded, "but please don't tell him that we were asking questions. We're trying to help his family."

"That's awful nice of you showfolks," the guard reacted. "If Booker needs money, I hope that you will let me contribute."

"We'll get back to you if the need arises," Sue assured him.

"Where do you think we can find him?" Debbie asked.

"I don't know where he is working right now, but he usually brings us a little treat just before the end of the late show. You might have seen him. He's most times in the hallway when you folks get off work. You girls working tonight?"

"No," Sue said. "This is our night for charity work. But don't spread it around. We like to work anonymously."

"I appreciate what you are saying and God bless you for it."

When the women were down the hall, Debbie could not resist. "So now you are Saint Susan of the showgirls. Why did you have to tell Gus that?"

"I had to say something!" Sue defended. "It's our cover story for asking questions. You should be proud of the way I can think on my feet."

"Sometimes I think our brains are in our feet," Debbie lamented. "What do we do now?"

"We go home, get some rest, and come back in disguise to see what Uncle Booker does after the show."

"What disguise?" Debbie asked. "We're six-foot showgirls! What do we know about being inconspicuous?"

"You're the one who wanted to play detective," Sue chided. "We'll come up with something."

CHAPTER EIGHTEEN

It took only one stop at the largest theatrical costumer in Vegas to outfit Sue and Debbie as a couple of grey-haired ladies on vacation. The wigs, the sunglasses, the baggy dresses that diminished their figures, and the flat canvas shoes were like a beauty makeover gone wrong. The final touches were sweater vests that could be justified in their roles as slot machine junkies who stayed in the air-conditioned casinos all day.

"Take the makeup down a few pegs and find a full-cup bra and we look like we just got off the bus," Sue said as she looked in the mirror.

"All we need now is an ugly purse and a big cup of quarters," Debbie agreed.

The late show started at 10:30 and ran for an hour and forty minutes, so the girls had until midnight to get into position to watch Ramon enter the casino from the staff service hallway. If they were right, Uncle Booker would be close behind. They had formulated no plan beyond surveillance, except that they would go home if they had guessed wrong.

They spotted Ramon as he came out the door with crew and cast members. Most of them would be going home or out to eat. They knew that Ramon would probably leave the Tropicana and make his way up The Strip where he would not have the burden of being seen as an employee. It looked as if he were heading for the lobby exit where he could get a taxi.

At first they did not see Booker. Like them, the uncle had anticipated Ramon's movements and was already in the casino. Sue saw him first, while Debbie was still focused on the staff exit door.

"There he is," Sue said with excitement as she tugged at Debbie's vest. "He is following Ramon."

Sue and Debbie had several significant advantages over Anglo in the game of surveillance. First, they knew Las Vegas, especially The Strip, as well as a teenager knows his own neighborhood. They knew the casino entrances, the layouts, the taxi stands and the side streets. Secondly, there were two of them to split up and cover the subject's possible movements. And, finally, there was the communication advantage; each girl carried a cellular phone with push-button automatic dialing to her partner's number.

By keeping at least one row of slot machines between them and the man known as Booker, they had concealment from which to follow him. When Ramon led the uncle across open areas, they, like him, skirted around the edges of the spaces so as to blend into the movers and players.

Ramon bypassed the cab stand, took the overhead walkway across Tropicana to the east side of Las Vegas Boulevard, and continued walking past the MGM Grand to the Aladdin. The girls lost sight of Ramon on the semi-crowded street, but they were able to keep pace with the uncle without being compromised.

Most Las Vegas restaurants close by midnight, but there are always food and beverage outlets open in the casinos. Ramon stopped at a raised, open, terrace-like restaurant in Aladdin for a meal. From their position behind the slot machines, the girls could see Ramon clearly while also keeping an eye on the uncle, who sat at a table in the sports book betting area. To further their cover, Debbie began to feed quarters into a slot machine.

His meal complete, Ramon was on the move again and so was the uncle. Sue had just said "let's go" when Debbie's machine started ringing a jackpot. Quarters began their metallic staccato against the stainless steel payoff bin as Sue pulled Debbie away from the machine.

"That's twenty-five dollars!" Debbie protested, as she reached out plaintively.

"Let it go," Sue commanded. "Do you want to lose them?"

Ramon played Blackjack at the Aladdin and then moved onto Bally's for two hours at a Let-It-Ride table. From their observation point, the girls could not tell if he was winning or losing. They used the stop to take turns in the ladies room and to have cocktails brought to them at the slots. Debbie continued to play a machine to keep their position, but she was losing about $30 an hour.

It was after 3 a.m. when the two middle-aged men approached them.

"You gals got to be prematurely grey because you are both beautiful," one of them said as an opening.

The girls flashed automatic smiles before they realized what they had encouraged.

"We've been admiring you from afar, as they say, for the last half-hour," the second one added. "I said to Al, maybe these ladies are unescorted. Maybe they would appreciate some male company. You know, for drinks, have a little fun, that type of thing."

"We got plenty of quarters," Al added.

"We're married," Sue said as a defensive measure.

"So are we," Al laughed. "Hey, that was never a reason to spoil a good time."

"She means that we are married to each other," Debbie lied.

The alcohol-aided grins slipped off the faces of both men, and they looked at each other as if the women were no longer present.

"Lesbos," Al pronounced.

"It's a sick world," the other replied. "Let's call it a night."

As the men moved off, Sue offered her hand to Debbie. "You are quick, girl. Best put-off I have ever seen. Congratulations."

The rest of the morning heading toward dawn was uneventful. Ramon moved to Caesar's Palace, where he gambled briefly and then talked to the girls serving out of a bar with few customers. Although Ramon seemed familiar with the cocktail waitresses, Sue and Debbie could detect no threatening attachments.

Without warning, the uncle walked out of Caesar's and took a taxi back to Paradise Village. The girls followed, took up station until Ramon ran into view, and then departed. They concluded that they had established the pattern.

"If he follows Ramon, then he follows us, too, on the nights we go out together," Debbie said on the ride home.

"I know," Sue agreed. "We've got to confront him. That's all there is to it."

"Where? When?" Debbie asked.

"I don't know yet. But unless we get some sleep, we're going to have puffy eyes and rubber legs for today's shows."

"Yeah," Debbie teased. "We wouldn't want Al and his friend to see us like that, would we?"

The showgirls waited two days before they confronted Anglo. They had decided not to tell Ramon about being followed until they knew why. The time and place that they chose was after the late show in the safety of the Tropicana.

When the finale curtain closed, Sue and Debbie raced to their dressing room to get out of costume and into street clothes. They removed their false eyelashes and wigs, but had no time to replace their show makeup. They had to get to the casino area outside the cast exit and spot Booker before Ramon changed and started out. They wanted to intercept Uncle Booker in the casino before he could follow Ramon out of the building.

They were relieved when they spotted the old man standing against a wall beyond the sightline of cast members using the exit. They anticipated Ramon's movement to the lobby exit and positioned themselves to intercept the uncle after Ramon had passed. The plan worked.

Anglo unexpectedly found his path blocked by two tall young women. When he tried to excuse himself and move around them, they moved with him to further block his forward progress.

"We know who you are, Mr. Booker, Indian Uncle, or whatever you are," Sue announced.

"And we know that you have been following Ramon, too," Debbie added.

"Who are you?" Anglo asked in surprise.

"We're Ramon's best friends," Sue said. "We work with him in the show so don't make trouble or we will call security."

Anglo paused to rein in his galloping mind. He relaxed to regain his center so that he might see the two women with clarity. He looked into their intense eyes seeking not motivation but connection.

"Well?" Sue demanded. "Why are you following Ramon?"

"I would like to explain," Anglo said softly. "Can we find a quiet place to talk?"

The girls led Anglo to an open-area casino bar where most tables were only a rail away from the passing public. Their table was as far from the rail as possible, but still in full view of the bar staff, who acknowledged the showgirls when they came in.

"We are known here," Sue warned, "so don't start anything."

"I apologize for causing you concern," Anglo began. "I am following Ramon because I don't know what else to do."

"Get a life," Debbie said without mercy.

"Are you an employee here?" Sue probed.

"No," Anglo replied. "I try to be helpful so that I can be close to Ramon."

"Why?" Sue demanded.

"Because Ramon is Dancer, is White Wing, a treasure that seems lost to his people. I am sent to find a way to restore him."

"They are going to kidnap him," Debbie accused with alarm.

"No," Anglo said calmly. "That is not our way."

"So you want Ramon to go back to the reservation," Sue confirmed.

"Yes."

Sue retorted. "Well, how stupid can that be?
I've seen pictures of how Indians live on the reservation. It's like living in a third-world country.
No jobs. Crummy housing. Poor food. Don't Indians become alcoholics and kill themselves more
than any other ethnic group?"

"Much of what you say is true," Anglo admitted.

"Then why do you want to take Ramon back
to that?" Sue did not wait for Anglo to answer.
"Ramon can make over $100,000 a year here and
live out every man's fantasy. He wears the best
clothes, goes to the best places and gets treated
like a star. What else could he want? He came
here with nothing but his talent, and now he
has everything."

"Is that so?" Anglo asked.

"Does he know that you are here to take him
back to the reservation?" Debbie demanded.

"No."

"Well, why haven't you asked him?"

"Our people believe that there is a right time
for every question and a sign to indicate every
right time."

"You've been following Ramon looking for a
sign?" Debbie asked in disbelief.

"That is a fair way of looking at it," Anglo
agreed.

"But you are not even an Indian," Sue said.
"You are a white man. What is in it for you?"

"The salvation of the world," Anglo answered
simply.

"Oh, oh," Debbie exclaimed, throwing up her hands with the long painted false nails. "If it isn't the perverts, it's the religious creeps."

Sue ignored the comment. "You're serious about this, aren't you?"

"Yes. If you would like to know, I will try to tell you why Ramon is so important to all of us."

"You are talking heavy stuff, aren't you?" Sue asked.

"The heaviest," Anglo confirmed.

"I don't think we are ready to hear it," Sue said seriously.

"I understand," Anglo replied.

"What are you two talking about?" Debbie demanded.

"Be quiet a minute," Sue instructed, and then she turned back to Anglo. "We seem to be working at cross-purposes."

"Is that so?" Anglo asked.

"Yes, I think so. You are on a holy mission for the Indians. You want Ramon to live like a monk to satisfy some primitive belief system. I want Ramon to be free to grab all he can from a very selfish, mean environment. Here he can join the real world, the modern world. What you offer is poverty and failure."

"Is that so?" Anglo asked.

"I think it is," Sue confirmed.

"Will you give me an opportunity to show you who Ramon really is?" Anglo asked.

"Why?"

"So that you can satisfy your own mind and be free from conflict."

"You mean know that we have done the right thing?"

"Exactly," Anglo said.

"And how do you propose we do this?" Sue asked with interest.

"Let us come together with Ramon, who is known among the tribes as Dancer, and let him dance."

"We've seen him dance plenty of times," Debbie interjected.

"You have not seen him dance in the spirit. Neither have I. I would like to see this. You should see this."

"How?" Sue's curiosity peaked.

"There is Red Rock Canyon and Valley of Fire. Either place is appropriate. I have a drum and can sing for him to dance."

"This is nuts," Debbie said.

"No," Sue corrected. "This could be very interesting. We'll do a picnic at Red Rock Canyon and see what happens."

"What do we tell Ramon?" Debbie asked.

"We tell him nothing for the time being," Sue replied pensively. "We'll say we met you, Uncle Booker, one day when we dropped by Ramon's apartment. We'll say that we are changing our strategy and trying to get to know you. We'll get Ramon, Dancer, to dance and try it your way. But if we don't change our minds, we want you to leave town."

"That is not a promise I can make," Anglo replied.

"Look," Sue insisted. "It's our way or the highway. You wouldn't stand a chance with Ramon if we worked against you. At least this way, you get a hearing. It's got to be better than sneaking around waiting for a sign."

"Perhaps you are the sign," Anglo said.

"We're no sign. We're just a couple of showgirls looking out for number one."

"Is that so?"

CHAPTER NINETEEN

The dreams of Indians are distinct from the dreams of whites. Persons raised in western cultures do not dream themselves as animals. In Native American contemplation, the dreamer may take the form of a coyote and feel the excitement of its running. In Indian dreams, humans have voices, but so do animals, trees, and stones.

Dancer had once enjoyed a rich dream life. His favorite retreat was a narrow dream canyon where the sheer vertical walls contained the cool, strange light of shadows, and where a deep azure sky ran like a river overhead. The powder sand floor was an inviting bed where silence gave rise to visions.

Visions in Indian life confirm an individual's movement toward doing the will of the Great Spirit. They are recognitions of devotion that direct life's path. The presence of the vision is more important than its interpretation. Often the symbols are confusing. Sometimes the vision requires no action. The sacred moment in itself is enough.

White Wing created in his dancing the Indian metaphor for existence. He danced within the Medicine Wheel. Beginning in the heart, the center, he could dance to the four directions and to the up above and the down below. He could dance the four seasons and feel the vibrations of the four colors. The mental, emotional, physical, and spiritual aspects of himself merged. In dancing he could experience the whole of it in the length of a single drum song. He danced the vision circle within the circle for understanding, for peace, and for vitality beyond fear.

Once White Wing had lived time in the cycles normally associated with nature. There was a steady internal rhythm to living that connected him to the earth and to the movements of the sun, the moon, and the stars. In Las Vegas, material progress had flattened time to a linear continuum on which all things were quantitatively measured. The progress mentality assumed that whatever came earlier on the linear scale was somehow inferior to the more recent, or to those things which would arise in the future. The idea allowed for no center of permanence. It engendered only an ever-increasing alienation from nature.

For Dancer, the natural cycle had been the circle in which he experienced fulfillment. Las Vegas filled the void within him with its values. It flaunted pleasure. It built its success by gambling on the future. It would risk everything on a roll of dice or the spin of a mechanical wheel.

Dancer had ventured too far into its rapids and now he was caught up in the tumultuous churning of its traffic and lights.

There was, however, a constant sense of alienation within Dancer. Although he had gained acceptance at the Tropicana, and he moved among the whites and participated in their social and sexual rituals, Dancer remained the observer.

The condition of the collective world that he saw was confusing. He witnessed no respect for others in the acts and the speech of those he encountered. Respect was not a feeling or an attitude in Indian culture; it was their way of living with each other. The false respect that he saw postured in Las Vegas was based on fear, not on trust.

Dancer, like every Indian, had internalized the defeat of his people. Many reservation Indians were still no more than prisoners of war. They both hated and feared the people and the government who had committed genocide against them. And yet, Dancer felt that he had now counted coup on the whites with his victory in Las Vegas. He had come among them as a lone warrior. He had made them applaud his feats of strength and agility. He had even taken some of their women. He had made them respect him where they gave no respect to each other. He had discovered that they were not superior to his people. The Shoshonis had named the whites barbarians in their language. The Cree word for the whites meant the helpless ones. The Sioux word for them was monsters. The Crows and Cheyennes referred to them as yellow-eyes. The Blackfeet, seeing their beards, called them bear faces. From what Dancer had observed in Las Vegas, the original names still applied.

The life of a solitary warrior was lonely and filled with sacrifice, Dancer admitted. The worst of it was that the city stole his dreams. It was a dark pit that swallowed visions and did not allow them to arise. The dancing that he performed at the Tropicana was no vision vehicle. It had been corrupted, and in a way Dancer was glad. The audiences were not worthy of seeing his worship. They could not come into the circle of his visions. Twelve times a week he insulted them, and in their ignorance they cheered their own humiliation. By this rationalization, Dancer replaced his own fear with contempt.

In the place of dreams which had visionary content, Dancer dreamed from the ego where he achieved fame in its thousand forms. He dreamed the white man's dreams of material success and power over others. He dreamed of returning to his people as a hero who had conquered the white society. He dreamed of telling the stories of counting coup among the whites, of his victories and their humiliations. He dreamed that he would endure in tribal mythology as the Indian who beat the whites on their own unholy ground.

It would take years, Dancer thought, maybe even a lifetime, but he would show them.

CHAPTER TWENTY

When the heat of the Las Vegas summer becomes drastic, tourists, and even local residents, seek cooler environs. Locals know that when the thermometer goes over the hundred mark, the temperature in their parked cars can reach 165 degrees. Cassette tapes and lipsticks melt. From noon until 7 p.m. dehydration, sunburn, and cancer-causing ultraviolet radiation reign. The best time of day to be outdoors is between 2 and 5 a.m.

Many of the big production shows on The Strip stayed dark one, or even two nights a week in recognition of the slow hottest weeks. Most of the performers welcomed the break, although they did not want to go out into the heat any more than their absent audiences did.

The girls wondered how Ramon had tolerated a virtual stranger in his house for three weeks without complaint. When asked, Ramon shrugged his shoulders and said that a guest accepted could not be turned out. He seemed unaware of the weeks that had passed.

"I wouldn't let my own mother stay three weeks," Debbie noted.

Ramon accepted the change in strategy for dealing with Anglo without comment. It both pleased and bewildered the women. They were pleased that he followed their judgments, but they were also bewildered by how little he seemed affected by them.

"You can never tell what is going on in his head," Debbie complained. "Sometimes I wish that he would argue with us. He could say, like, 'I'm not going to pay for another Armani suit' or 'I refuse to go out with women over 65,' but it seems whatever we want is OK by him."

"Maybe none of those things are important to him," Sue speculated. "I'll bet you that he could be unmovable if he wanted to be."

"Yeah, he's the Indian Clark Kent, mild-mannered and all of that until he runs into a phone booth."

Red Rock Canyon is a National Conservation Area of 83,100 acres located 20 miles west of Las Vegas. There is a one-way 13-mile scenic drive that loops through the major geologic features in the upper third of the preserve. About 65 million years ago, two crustal plates collided, forming gray limestone mountains and younger, massive red sandstone boulders similar to those in the Valley of Fire. The red rocks have attracted human investment since the earliest men discovered them.

The site for the sunrise outing was the Willow Spring Picnic Area on the backside of the scenic drive. Sue subverted the entrance gate to gain access to the road before the normal daylight opening hours. She had had some romantic dates at Willow Spring during more favorable times of the year, and at better hours, but at least she felt comfortable about the seven-mile, pitch-black route.

"As long as we don't hit one of the wild burros, we will be all right," Sue advised. "They like to stand on the road, hoping that the tourists will feed them."

The headlights of the BMW yielded only hints of the red rock massifs as they passed the Calico Hills observation points. In daylight, most visitors stopped here to take photos and to hike into the rocks, which climbed in accessible but deceiving pathways. The perspective made the formations seem so near, but climbers appeared as ants after laboring an hour on the rock faces.

From the time the girls picked up the men at Ramon's apartment, they made conversation rather than face the silence of the wooden Indians in the backseat.

"Since we usually have supper at one in the morning and breakfast at two in the afternoon," Sue said to the backseat, "I wasn't sure what to bring for a sunrise picnic. I told Room Service to use their imagination. All I know is that we have two coolers of something in the trunk.

They are heavy, so I don't think that we will be disappointed."

"We gave them some comps to the show and a nice tip," Debbie added. "It better be good."

Anglo sat next to Ramon with his Taos hand drum in his lap. He wore boots, jeans, the black and green T-shirt with the petroglyph design given to him by the Silvas, and his blanket in a narrow fold over his right shoulder. His western-style summer hat would have hit the ceiling liner of the car if he had not stayed slightly bent. The leather drum cover containing ritual items lay at his feet.

Dancer's reservation and road clothes had been confiscated by the two women at the time of his makeover. His most casual attire now consisted of snakeskin boots, beige linen trousers and a burgundy, silk short-sleeved shirt. He wore no hat. Although Dancer knew that Anglo had requested a sunrise ceremonial dance, he had brought none of his personal accouterments for ritual. These items remained in a battered piece of luggage in the closet of his room. He had decided that he would dance to please the women and to show respect for Anglo, but he planned it only as a gesture. For the same reasons that he had refused to dance at local powwows, Dancer avoided the reminders of his previous self.

When they arrived at Willow Spring, Sue selected a picnic area and the men unloaded the car in the light of its headlamps. Anglo spread his blanket on the ground and sat facing the rim of the Calico Hills over which the sun would rise. He removed the drum beater, a ceremonial rattle, and an eagle feather fan from the drum bag and placed them on the blanket. Sue turned off the car lights and the darkness enveloped them.

Sue and Debbie stayed near Ramon at the picnic table. Sue was just about to speak to fill the void of silence when Anglo began a soft, steady drumbeat. The drum reverberated in waves that seemed to touch her skin and she dared not break its spell. Debbie, who was more likely to make an aside, was also speechless.

The drum continued and then Anglo began to sing. The effect in the total darkness was chilling and wonderful at the same time to the women. They had never heard anything like it. Anglo seemed to be summoning the sun to appear, and within minutes the sky began to lighten. Soon the peaks of the Calico Hills were silhouetted against the horizon. Then, dim light spilled into the valley and the women could discern Anglo from the darkness. Dancer left their side and crossed the open ground to Anglo's blanket, where he picked up the fan and the rattle. They heard the sharp, short sounds of the shaken rattle keeping time with the drum before they saw the dance movements.

The women did not know what to expect from the dance, as they had only seen Ramon perform the wildly energetic Fancy Dance. As the light revealed more, Dancer seemed to be greeting the new sun with the eagle feather fan. He held the plumes aloft to the sun's first rays and then moved the fan as if to bathe his head and upper body, all the while keeping rhythm with the heroic sun-greeting song Anglo was singing. Dancer's body was erect. His movements, consisting of short forward and side steps, were dignified, even reverent. Both women, who had practiced every dance from ballet to tap, were struck by the power and stateliness of Dancer's movements. Each step had Dancer balanced on the balls of his feet, the heel of the lead foot barely striking the ground on every drumbeat. It was as if the rays of the sun were strings up-lifting the man and freeing him from the weight of earth. The familiar song and the heartbeat of the drum had in the same moment freed Dancer's mind from thought. He had gone to that spirit place between the drumbeats that was evidenced by the expression of ecstasy in his eyes. In recognition of the privilege and awe that they felt, each woman spontaneously reached out to the other and the two joined hands.

The song continued until the great orb of life itself appeared and its warmth was felt on their faces. The drum and the song grew in intensity until on a final beat both singer and dancer stopped simultaneously. Dancer handed the fan and the rattle to Anglo and then turned and walked away from the picnic area without saying a word.

By the time Dancer returned, Sue and Debbie had unpacked their morning repast and displayed it on the picnic table. One cooler was packed with four platters on ice: one of elaborately presented fresh fruits; one of cut vegetables around a generous cup of dip; one of cheeses and slices of turkey, ham and roast beef laid out carefully around mustard and mayonnaise condiments with three types of bread; and finally a platter of large cocktail shrimp displayed around a deep plate of red cocktail sauce. The second cooler had a compartment filled with ice, with four splits of white wine and four bottles of spring water. A second compartment contained four splits of red wine, a thermos of coffee and the plates, cups, silverware and napkins necessary for service.

"It pays to have connections," Debbie said with pride as she offered the spread to the men.

The hour after dawn was still pleasant and alive with the rustle of nocturnal feeders in the brush. The party congregated around the picnic table to enjoy the feast, but there was little conversation. When Anglo had finished his plate, Sue took the opportunity to put her arm through his and lead him down the unpaved road that led to Red Rock Summit.

"I wanted to thank you for a beautiful morning," Sue began. "Seeing and hearing you and

Ramon is an experience I will never forget. For a few moments, I had the feeling that the whole world was your church. I understand now why you wanted us to see Ramon dance in this way."

"He is a very special soul," Anglo said.

"Why do you say that?"

"I say that because ceremonial dance is a very high form of worship among the Pueblo people. Talent alone will not take one to the level White Wing has achieved. It has nothing to do with winning contests. White Wing carries within his dance the legacy of mankind's vital tie with the Earth. He is the walking metaphysic of nature. If we lose his gift, humankind erases one pathway back to sanity. We lose our understanding of how to exist on the Earth. Dancer carries not only spiritual truth, but physical truth as well."

"My God," Sue said, "you were serious when you told us he was the salvation of the Earth. I didn't think you meant it literally. Do you actually believe that Ramon is the Christ or something?"

"No, White Wing is not that, but he has the same potential for expressing Truth. He is part of a tradition of holy men going back thousands of years into a time when the human species was not separate from creation. In the Pueblo tradition, the memory of unseparated existence is carried by the cacique, the tribal holy man. The tribe's current cacique and the tribal Elders believe that Dancer is the chosen one for the continuation of their traditional life. If not White Wing, who? Who can become the next generation cacique?"

"Well," Sue rationalized, "there must be other candidates."

"In all that remains of the 500 Indian Nations, there are few individuals worthy of this trust. White Wing, by his childhood association with tribal Elders and his devotion to ceremonial dance, is a very rare treasure."

"And so you think Debbie and I are leading Ramon to hell," Sue said bitterly.

"I cannot judge you. Dancer has chosen his own path. We cannot judge him either."

"So what are you going to do?"

"I need do nothing. That is the most difficult discipline. We do not impose our will on others. We wait—"

"Yes, I know," Sue interrupted. "You wait for a sign. You wait for the right time and the right words. It doesn't seem like a very efficient way to run a railroad."

"Ah," Anglo smiled. "Where are the railroads now?"

Sue was puzzled for a moment, but then she saw the joke. "Gee, you have a sense of humor, and here I thought you were some kind of stone Buddha."

"The Buddha laughs," Anglo replied.

Sue smiled again. "You don't see me and Debbie as your enemies, do you?"

"Of course not."

"I'm glad, but that doesn't mean that we are going to help you with Ramon. He has a right to live any lifestyle that he wants."

"Of course," Anglo agreed.

"So you want to stay in Las Vegas?"

"Yes."

"OK," Sue said. "We can live with that."

CHAPTER TWENTY-ONE

"I have been in Las Vegas for eleven months," Dancer began, "and this is the first time that I have danced for myself."

These were the first personal words Dancer had spoken to Anglo. The two men had entered the apartment a few minutes before, after returning from Red Rock Canyon. Anglo sat on the sofa and acknowledged Dancer with his eyes as the younger man paced the width of the room.

"It is difficult being me," Dancer continued with a mock laugh. "I am uneasy in my own skin."

"I know that place," Anglo said.

"How is it that you sing our songs and practice our ways?"

"It is the gift of Nita, and Joseph, and Carlos, and the Elders. They took me in when I was empty and showed me the way to be full."

"This seems impossible to me," Dancer said, shaking his head.

"The cool water of a mountain stream does not deny itself to those who thirst. Why then should the Great Spirit deny vision to those who seek it?"

"You sound like an Indian priest or a medicine man," Dancer accused.

"Those words honor me, but I do not have the preparation for such high office. You already know and have experienced more than I can ever learn in the years left to me. You can lead. You can teach. I am still at the edge of the Circle. You have danced at its center."

"And what has it gotten me?" Dancer said with some bitterness. "I'm the National Champion Fancy Dancer, and everything that I owned from dancing powwows could be carried in two hands. My friends are alcoholics who count the number of car crashes that they have survived like real warriors used to count battles. The reservations are poorhouses where our people wait out their lives on government handouts. Most Indians don't understand or even practice their own rituals. What is the point of continuing?"

"Should an eagle become a snake?" Anglo asked in quiet, even tone.

"Eagles were killed almost to extinction," Dancer retorted with force.

"Would you like to hear what I have observed about Indian people and this land?" Anglo asked.

"Is this a government school lecture or a white religious sermon? If it is, I don't want to hear it."

"I don't believe that it is."

"Then I will listen."

"The Native Americans listened for the voice of the Great Spirit in every animal, tree, and stone upon the land. The white man, the anglos, and the Spanish told you that they talked to God with their prayers. They looked to the sky and begged His favor, but did not keep silent for His answer. They talked. God was supposed to listen. When did they listen?

"Now your people have forgotten how to listen. The errors of the whites have deafened them with hatred. They hear their own suffering and misery, generations of it carried in their blood, and they can hear nothing else.

"Even in the trance of the drum, the singing and the dancing into the sacred world, they return and do not realize where they have been. They know that they feel alive, and free, and powerful, but they do not remember the Source. If they did, would they then spend the rest of the night in a quest for alcohol and sex? Would an eagle choose to become a snake?

"What would this land be today if the white man had understood what you had to share? Suppose he had learned your ways of listening for the voice of the Great Spirit in every animal, tree, and stone. Suppose your sacred mountains and rivers had become sacred to him as well? Suppose he had valued you as nations worth understanding rather than territories for plundering? What would this land be today?

"And what can it become without you? How can it survive without the natives who tended its nature so closely that it became their own? What if you, the keepers of its sacredness, forget the places and the ways of its vitality? If its Spirit dies within you does it, too, die?

"I say to you, my new blood, and to the remnants of the 500 tribal nations, Ya hey, return to your heart. Put down the bottle, and the dice. You have holy work to do. Only you carry the seeds of a righteous land. It is in your blood. Many kin have died so that you might live to carry this seed. Do not waste your life. Seek your vision as a great warrior of the Spirit. Find the gift within you and give it away. The greatest honor goes to the giver of gifts, for when it seems that he has nothing left to give, he has attained everything. The gift you have to give is water to the thirsty. It is fire to the chilled. It is food to the starving.

"If you share my blood, come back to the circle. Take off your hard shoes and wear again the moccasins of your forefathers. Take up the rattle and the eagle feather fan and move your feet in time with the drum. Give up your cares in the world outside the circle and sing with us the old chants that free our minds and leave us receptive to His presence."

Anglo was speaking as in a trance, as if the words were already written and his only need was the opening of his mouth. Dancer stood dumbfounded, rooted to the spot in motionless attention. In the Pueblo culture of short discourses, Anglo's speech continued as a flood in a dry river bed.

"Then bring another into the circle, making each a blood brother and sister until there is no one left outside. Sing the vocables that transcend any language. Everyone can sing. Everyone can dance. Everyone can feel the vibration that connects us all; every man, every woman, every animal, every tree, every rock. And thus we become the water rushing in a mountain stream and the soaring of the eagle reflected in a sunflecked pool. We become the all. We knew this once as a people. It is essential that we know this again.

"This is the historic hour of Indian destiny. You who are poor and forgotten, who have suffered every anguish, misery, and indignity man can invent, you now hold the seeds of a nation's salvation.

"It is not a religion that you have to give. It is beyond religion. Let every member of the nation come into your circle and experience his own vision. Do not say what the vision may be, or what it should be. Any vision which arises from within the circle is honored. No rank prevails.

"The Great Spirit speaks to all who will listen. The only precondition is humility. The only talent required is a quiet mind. The circle is a holy symbol. The drum, the singing and dancing, are only methods. The apparent frenzy leads to inner peace, an absolute silence where only spirit exists. This is the goal. It has always been the goal. For thousands of years, around incalculable campfires and drums, humankind has strived to reconnect with its Source.

"I say to you, White Wing, that modern man is far removed from Creation. Yet, the yearning is always present. The inner self wants to be restored to its origins. It wants to go home. This home is the same for all life. Human cultures have confused the issue, but reunion is the same destination for us all no matter how it is pictured.

"Perhaps time is the place where we live out each individual life there ever was in order to understand the truth of the interconnection. Only after we have experienced being everyone and everything will we be satisfied with creation. This is what the ego seems to require."

Anglo stopped talking and the room was silent for long minutes.

"No one has ever spoken to me in this way," Dancer finally said.

"I have not spoken so long in my life," Anglo admitted. "It began and I myself did not know its course or its end. Did I stretch the tail of the muskrat?"

"No," Dancer replied. "Much of what you said was a story I know to be true. But I can't believe that it is my destiny to save the white man."

"Not just the white man, all men. Not just you, but all Native Americans who have your experience."

"I can't carry that burden. I won't," Dancer protested. "I won't sacrifice my life for some crazy ideal."

"The only way we can come together in this moment is for you to live my life and for me to live yours. Perhaps in the cycle of time that will occur," Anglo concluded.

"Count on having a long wait," Ramon said. "I have better things to do."

Ramon gathered some personal items from his bedroom and left the apartment without another word.

Anglo remained seated on the sofa, his eyes closed, regretting the flood he had loosed on Dancer, wondering how he had once held the dam on so many ideas.

CHAPTER TWENTY-TWO

For the first time since his arrival, although he had touched the bag each morning in his sunrise ritual, Anglo opened the medicine bag and held each item as a means of gathering strength and guidance. His mind, in its unwanted discourse, had accused Anglo of blundering in his first personal moments alone with Dancer. Like the white man that he is, it said, Anglo had reverted to type and pushed the hard sell. The white man had decided what was right and what was logical and then had trumpeted his case in one great effort of sound and fury.

The mind was full of recriminations that speculated on dire consequences. It was an undisciplined naysayer whose existence depended on its ability to separate being from creation. Winn Conover had discovered the peaceful effects of tethering his mind from its marauding tendencies. Gradually he had corralled the beast and lulled it into calm. Only then had Winn been free to become Booker Washington Jones. And as Booker discovered that state of consciousness beyond the limits of the mind, he became Anglo. Now all this passage was threatened by the revival of accusatory thoughts. The mind is a jealous companion who demands first place in the affections of awareness.

Anglo retreated into ritual as a barrier against thoughts. Ritual could subdue the mind and leave the path open to vision. But for Anglo it was a struggle that required a warrior's energy, a warrior's courage, and a warrior's heart. He would not be required to cut off a finger to the knuckle, as vision quest warriors had done in the past, but he would suffer. He would suffer the threat of failure, a pain so severe that it caused killing heart attacks and strokes in the white men of his generation. Anglo fought off depression and the bodily poisons it generated with ritual. He had never felt so vulnerable.

In the days after the Red Rock Canyon sunrise, Anglo stopped following Dancer, although he kept the performer's hours as a way of being available to him. On the early mornings when Dancer returned to the apartment and passed Anglo sitting outside on the veranda, he spoke a civil greeting, but seemed disinclined to conversation. In the afternoons when Dancer awoke for his work, he busied himself with grooming and dressing and then left the apartment with only the most formal of acknowledgments to his guest. In an entire month, Anglo had spoken at length only once to Dancer, and the result seemed counterproductive to his mission. How could Anglo make a progress report to Joseph and the Elders? How could he return to Santa Fe and justify or explain his failure? Anglo saw no other option but to remain in Las Vegas.

Dancer continued the routine of his Las Vegas lifestyle, but he often heard the echoes of Anglo's words. Dancer had never considered that he could initiate a purpose to his life.

For Dancer the streets and the architectural landscape of Las Vegas were a wasteland. No spirits of primordial origins were available for strength and guidance. There were no animals or awakening sites to reveal spiritual potentialities. He could find nothing sacred with which to identify. He realized that the sun-greeting dance at Red Rock Canyon had been a brief reconnection to his traditional self.

The Elders had told him to keep remembering or he would die. They had spoken of remembrance of the land as the way of tribal continuance. They had shown him sacred sites that were only visible to the inner eye. Dancer had felt their resonance and the experience had kept him loyal to the land. The ceremonies of everyday life also kept identification with the land. The Elders had warned White Wing to listen for the guiding voices of his ancestors who reside in the land, lest he get lost in the illusions of life.

Las Vegas was a very strong illusion. It was the symbol of excess and wantonness. It would risk everything for pleasure. It worshipped extravagance. It was unreasonable and wasteful in every attribute. It was also seductive to the selfish ambitions of the human mind to which it pandered relentlessly.

Las Vegas was a mechanical organism, endowed with the energy of greed that devoured young people like Ramon Ortiz irrespective of their cultural orientation. Its neon lights mesmerized until its carnal delights fractionalized every intent to be sane. If Red Rock Canyon stood for connection to the earth, then the Las Vegas skyline was its disenfranchisement.

Dancer was lost in the psychological landscape of Las Vegas. His internal compass, which pointed true in his homeland, was now fixed by the magnetism of the city to its own direction. Instead of finding his way out of the morass, he sank deeper into its intent.

If Anglo had followed him the week after Red Rock Canyon, he would have been led into downtown clubs where nude shows were presented and where seductresses danced into the wallets of their customers. But Anglo could not have followed him into the private room where Ramon paid a nude woman to sensually bathe him. It was as if Ramon were attempting to burn out the campfires of his tradition with the fires of sexual orgasm. The liquor and the sex subdued the internal voices. They quieted the questions which Dancer could not answer.

Then one morning, while Dancer slept the drugged sleep of excess, Anglo called a taxi and went shopping. By the time Dancer awoke, he could smell the food. It smelled like his mother's kitchen. When he stumbled into the living area, he saw Anglo at the stove monitoring pots of squash and beans and fresh hot peppers in a to-mato sauce. Fry bread had been rolled out on the bar top counter and the flour had spread accidentally to the seats of the bar stools.

"Could you check the corn?" Anglo asked. "It's on the veranda."

Dancer, not sure that he was not dreaming, opened the front door to the intense afternoon heat and smelled roasting corn. Outside in his robe, he inspected a smoker grill that he had never seen before. The price sticker was still vis-ible on its black dome top. When he lifted the lid, a rush of steam revealed ears of corn roast-ing in their own husks. He turned the corn with a set of implements, also still bearing their price stickers, and went back inside just in time to hear the first piece of fry bread crack in the hot oil.

Anglo felt the curiosity of his bewildered host as a prickling sensation on his back. He turned to respond.

"It's a good day to cook," he said.

Dancer shook his head in negative wonder and

left the room to take a shower. By the time he returned, Anglo was ready to serve the meal. Dancer filled his plate and began to eat without comment. He had a good appetite and took second helpings in tribute to the cook.

"You surprise me again," Dancer finally said. "The fry bread needs work, but everything else was very good."

"Since when can an Indian find perfect fry bread?" Anglo said with humor.

"That is true." Dancer allowed himself a broad smile.

"I have herbal tea from the pueblo. Maria, our kin, mixed it for this visit. Will you drink tea?"

"I will drink Maria's tea," Dancer said. "I will also smoke the pipe if it is offered."

"Good," Anglo responded.

The tastes from his home were undeniable. The peppers bit the tongue and flavored the squash. The corn, eaten off the cob in eagerness while it was still too hot, tasted of smoke and earth. Maria's tea spoke of the herbs Dancer had collected for his mother as a child. The pipe smoke gathered up the symbolism of the meal and made it a sacred event.

The men sat on the floor, close enough together to be able to pass the pipe.

"Why do you stay?" Dancer said to break a long silence.

"I need your help," Anglo replied.

"How is that?"

"I want to do something for our people, but I do not have the vision," Anglo said. "I believe that you know the way."

"I have nothing to show you, Uncle. I have trouble seeing my own way," Dancer said quietly.

"Perhaps we are on the same path and can help each other."

"I doubt that," Dancer said, turning away.

"Then let me serve you until the way is made clear."

"You want to serve me?" Dancer questioned in surprise.

"Yes," Anglo affirmed. "I can pay a share of the rent, cook, and clean."

"Stop!" Dancer demanded. "No Elder should serve a fool like me."

"Who sees the Elder, and who sees the fool?" Anglo asked. "I see only two kinsmen bound together in need. Who is to say whose need is greater and whose is lesser? Are we not of the same clan?"

Dancer could not respond for a long interval.

"Today you are more of an Indian than I am," Dancer admitted. "I have called you a pretend Indian as an insult and the words have turned against me. Now I am the pretend Indian who threatens to deny kinship, and you are the real Indian who honors tradition. Skin has nothing to do with it, does it?"

"I hope not," Anglo answered, "because you have done me great honor with your words. And by those words you have also honored yourself in wisdom. Joseph says that we teach and are taught in the same breath. I am beginning to see how that works."

"You are my guest," Dancer concluded. "I give you my pledge that I will be a better host."

CHAPTER TWENTY-THREE

The girls' conversation for the last week had centered on their experiences with Ramon and Uncle Booker at Red Rock Canyon. Sue told Debbie the gist of her private talk with the older man.

"So Ramon is like a runaway Indian prince," Debbie paraphrased, "and the tribe wants him back."

"No," Sue corrected. "It's more like he is Jesus, who decides that he doesn't want to be a savior."

"Well, who could blame him?" Debbie replied. "Look what the world does to saviors."

The limited show schedule and the summer heat had diminished the quality and quantity of their casino dates, but the showgirls enjoyed the time off. They caught up on *The Young and the Restless*, a television soap opera that they videotaped every weekday, and updated their local investments. Sue bought some antique end tables for her future dream house in Northern California, and Debbie planned a party at her house for one of the Folies dark nights.

"Only real people," Debbie insisted, as she penned the invitations. "No phonies."

"What do you want to do about the Uncle?" Sue asked.

"I like the guy. He will be perfect for Maxine. She'll talk beauty parlor gossip for hours and he will listen. I'm inviting him."

"I wonder if he would bring his drum and sing for us?" Sue asked.

"Oh, wouldn't that be a hoot! We could bring the lights down low and run some chills up their spines."

"You would have to be respectful," Sue warned. "It's a religious thing with them."

"We've had parties with Ouija boards before. A couple of years ago Betty did a seance. Remember what a hoot that was?"

"It's not the same thing."

"OK," Debbie agreed, "but let's ask him anyway."

Booker Jones was detained by Tropicana Security and was being processed for unlawful trespass, when the news of his arrest spread throughout the kitchen and catering departments. A stream of sous-chefs, busboys, waitresses, banquet supervisors, dock managers, and even a guard assigned to the stage door descended on the Security Office in Booker's defense.

"He's been helping us for weeks," a kitchen manager said. "How were we supposed to know he wasn't being paid? I want to hire the guy right now."

"Oh no," the loading dock night supervisor protested. "Booker is our man. We got first dibs."

"Well what am I supposed to do without him?" a banquet manager complained.

In the end, a personnel manager was summoned to the Security Office to sort out the dilemma. In the frustration of not being able to please any department, the personnel lady made a Solomonic decision.

"Mr. Jones will work as he has in the past except that he will punch the time clock as an employee. His job title will be Utility Swing Shift Food Handler. The day shift will do the paperwork. Now go back to work!"

The crowd of well-wishers escorted Booker through the hotel office corridor and down the service elevator into their domain. Every person shook his hand. They pretended not to notice the tears in his eyes. No one gave him instructions. They knew that he would find the place where he was most needed.

In the nights Dancer did not have business with Sue and Debbie, he sought out Anglo to see if he wanted to go to dinner. Dancer referred to Anglo as Uncle in public. He showed respect for his tribal name, which even in its short form was not to be spoken among non-Indians.

In Native American languages, words and

names have sacred power. The spoken word begins with breath, the essence of life itself. It proceeds from the center of a person's being nearest
the heart. Native people use words very carefully
because they know that the power of words af-
fects both the speaker and the hearer. Non-Indians seem to feel that silence should be filled
with talk. However they give little value to what
is said. Often they do not even hear what is
said because they are too anxious to speak their
own words. Companionship without talk is awkward, unnatural to their society.

Dancer and Anglo were comfortable around
each other without conversation. Whites observing them seated across from each other at a restaurant table would think them sullen or bored,
but they were keenly alert.

Anglo did not speak the language of his
pueblo although he knew many songs and their
meanings. He was also not yet fluent in Spanish.
English somehow seemed an inadequate, even im-
proper language for his Indian thoughts. The
daily discourse he had with Dancer in English
was functional, but it was not purposeful to his
mission. He recognized that he would have to
find a non-verbal means to reach Dancer.

Anglo thought about the companionship of a
human being with a horse or a dog. One does
not speak the language of the other and yet they
communicate at profound depths. There is love
and communion and commitment for which each

would risk his own life to save the other. What words have created this bond of trust and affection? Words are not necessary, Anglo concluded. Words were not necessary in his becoming Nita's son. Words cannot be made that will call a cacique to his path. Sacred words have power, but Anglo could remember no sacred words in the English language. Even the word "God" had lost its impact in interpretation. No wonder the ancient Jews wrote the sacred name of God in their language, but never spoke it.

CHAPTER TWENTY-FOUR

Before the whites claimed the sacred lands of the Native Americans, the consciousness of certain individuals within each tribe caused them to make vision quests. The decision to perform the vision quest ceremony often required a year of serious contemplation. In seeking a vision that would specify a spiritual path and activate spirit guides, the seeker was making a lifetime commitment.

The quest itself tested an individual's physical and mental endurance to the extreme. It was both frightening and dangerous. In some cases, quest participants came screaming off the ceremonial hill. A few went insane. A few died.

Anglo had read about traditional vision quests, and he was also aware that they had been corrupted into commercial experiences marketed by travel agents. Modern vision questers, even those with spiritual motivations, wanted instant fulfillment based on a cost-effective itinerary. They might fast for a day, remain awake all night in prayer, and consider that a sacrifice, but it was a mere gesture to the Indian reality. In the Indian world, the family of the vision quester would follow him or her to the base of the ceremonial mount and kiss the person goodbye, believing—knowing—that the loved one might not survive the ordeal. How many modern seekers would take that risk?

The wisdom and the path of life of caciques like Joseph, and all Indian medicine men, result from individual visions brought about by dedication and ritualized vision quests. There can be no partial measures. For them, there is a willingness to suffer physical death in the pursuit of spiritual life.

Anglo had experienced dream-like visions in the sweatlodge. His entry into Pueblo tribal life was a fourfold dream in which he was first a deer running with other deer, and then rain falling into a river flowing as rapids. Next Anglo felt himself to be a tree, where his extended arms were branches for birds and squirrels to make their homes; and finally he lay in a field and raised his arms as stalks of ripe corn. Joseph had told him at the time that he was "both the gift and the giver."

The experience had been profoundly joyful. Anglo did not realize until much later its impact on his Indian hosts. They knew that the vision was exceptional even for an Indian. In a white man, it became a remarkable event to be incorporated into the tribe's oral history.

Anglo had continued to find peace and contentment in the sweatlodge and in the kiva of his adopted tribe, but his visions were not as clear and powerful as the first one. Often in the sweatlodge or in pipe ceremonies held in the kiva, his prayer requests were simple and the guidance received was gentle and subconscious.

Dancer, Anglo realized, was at the second level of his life cycle, struggling to find meaning and purpose in his life. Black Elk, the Holy Man of the Oglala Sioux, had his great vision at the age of nine, but it took a lifetime for him to understand its symbols. He had lived through the tragic decades of the Custer battle, the Ghost Dance, and the Wounded Knee massacre, but felt that he had failed to save his people. Black Elk's vision is legendary, and his legacy important to all Indian people today. Anglo knew these facts and saw parallels to Dancer's conflict. Few people can hope to cross over into the spirit world, but that is the requirement for spiritual leadership. Someone in Dancer's generation must try.

Anglo felt that Dancer was capable of crossing over and returning. His entire life had been a preparation for the effort. Anglo trusted the Great Spirit to guide and protect Dancer through the vision quest, but how was the ceremony to be initiated? Dancer had to devoutly yearn for the experience. It could not be offered, or even suggested. Where was the sacred hill? What were the artifacts to be used? What was the precise ritual? Anglo did not know.

The Indians had taught Anglo that spirituality is a lifestyle. Each person on the Earth has a special gift given by the Creator. Life is lived as a responsibility to develop the gift for the benefit of the whole community. Anglo could not believe that Dancer's gift was destined to be trivialized in Las Vegas.

What Anglo did next was seemingly as irrational as when he walked away from his home in Norfolk in the nude. He went to work at the Tropicana as usual, but clocked out before Dancer could find him in the kitchens. If the cab driver had not recognized Booker Jones, he never would have accepted the fare to Red Rock Canyon after midnight. When Booker asked to be let out at the entrance road, the driver objected.

"It's pitch black out here," he said. "There ain't no traffic and nobody for miles. You ain't planning on doing something stupid, are you? 'Cause if you are, I don't want no part of it."

"I just need to be alone," Anglo said simply.

"Well, you got the perfect place for it," the driver said sarcastically.

"Will you pick me up at the Visitor Center an hour after sunrise?"

"Gee, Booker, it's a long way out here, and I got to deadhead all the way back."

Anglo handed the driver a $100 bill.

"On the other hand," the driver said as he accepted the bill, "I'm glad to do you the favor."

Anglo walked down the center of the loop roadway, around the closed gate, and on for about a mile and a half to Calico Vista II. The weeping began there. It began as tears of frustration and regret over his handling of the mission to Las Vegas and grew into a throat-gripping lament that racked his body convulsively. Anglo let go of his self-discipline and cried the salt tears of despair and failure. He fell to his knees in the sharp gravel of the parking area with hands either covering his face or pulling at his hair. He beseeched the moon and the stars and then wailed his recriminations back at them when they would not answer. Exhausted, he fell on the rough ground and wallowed uncontrollably as the stones tore at his flesh and clothing. He tasted blood in his mouth and welcomed the madness.

His mind opened all its doors into the past and the failures of Winn Conover were displayed to be lamented. Every scene of wrongness as a husband, a father, and a citizen came up for hurtful review. Then Anglo saw the poverty, misery, and abuse of the Indian peoples that he loved. He railed against the ignorance that oppressed them. He mourned the children of the physical and cultural massacres. For hours Anglo thrashed about on the ground beneath the red rock massifs in passionate lamentation. His weeping was concealed in inky darkness, his wailing absorbed by the silent stones. Perhaps his grief was felt by the creatures of the night, who paused in their tracks to acknowledge him, but he did not sense them. He felt alone. Solitary. Helpless. Finally, mercifully, Anglo had no more to give to his lament, and he lapsed into unconsciousness.

It seemed not a heroic figure lying dirty, bloody, and ragged on the sharp gravel ground. If a Park Ranger had found him, he might have first thought Anglo a murder victim. He might then have been alarmed to see the man stand up from the dead. Even Anglo himself did not understand the process of the lament. He did not know that he had performed a ritual sacred to the Indian people. Great Chiefs had made laments. Invincible in combat, they yet rent their garments and wept themselves into exhaustion. They grieved over the suffering of their people and their inability to stop it. They doubted themselves and cried out for relief. There is pain in responsibility. Yet there is relief in suffering's lament.

Anglo woke as the sun reached his rocky bed. His eyes were red and swollen. His mouth and throat ached and his lips and nostrils were encrusted. Dirt and blood, transferred from his rock-cut hands, streaked his face. His shirt was ripped and dirty. Most of its buttons were missing. He was very thirsty and had a severe headache. He looked miserable, but he felt strangely light and relieved. Seeing no one on the road, he urinated where he had slept and then began the walk to the Visitor Center, where he waited to be picked up by the taxi.

CHAPTER TWENTY-FIVE

Dancer was sleeping when Anglo got back to the apartment. The taxi driver had wanted to take him to the Sunrise Hospital emergency room, but Booker had talked him out of it. Rather than risk being seen by Dancer, Anglo bathed himself at the kitchen sink. The worst of the cuts were on his knees and the palms of his hands, but they would heal in a few days.

Anglo made himself a pot of herbal tea and drank two cups. Although there was pain to remind him of his ordeal, he felt perfectly calm. The lament had been a kind of cleansing of the mind, a deep purification of the subconscious where sweetgrass smoke could not reach. He did not analyze the experience or question its purpose. There was only one person who he would tell about this night. He would confide in Joseph and seek to understand its significance in the sanctity of the kiva.

Debbie's end-of-the-summer party was more like a family reunion than a stylish show business event. Instead of catering, the girls and their friends cooked their own specialties and created a pitch-in supper. Debbie raised her sculptured eyebrows when Uncle Booker volunteered to bring his own grill and roast corn-on-the-cob on her patio. Dancer was exempt from bringing a covered dish, but Debbie did secure his promise to "sing Indian songs" with his uncle as the featured entertainment.

Debbie's two-bedroom home was stylishly furnished. It had been the developer's model, and she had bought it complete with pictures on the walls, knick-knacks on the lamp tables, and silverware in the kitchen drawers. The property was landscaped, but in place of a green lawn there was crushed white marble with painted cement statuary as accents. One of the subdivision rules was that residents had to park their vehicles in their garages. Unless there were guests, there was no on-street parking, often no evidence of life. The area was handsome, with wide landscaped boulevards whose unnatural trees and bushes flourished by virtue of automated sprinkler systems, but the adobe-styled architecture seemed sterile, cramped, and conformist. The houses were promoted as low maintenance, which appealed to several generations of homeowners with an aversion to yard work.

The party began at 8 p.m. with the arrival of guests and the laying out of the buffet. Wine, cocktails, and snacks were offered, and Debbie had her CD player programmed with happy, up-tempo albums by Hootie and the Blowfish, Bob Marley, Paul Simon, and Sting to provide background atmosphere. After supper, she planned a more romantic, mellow mood with Mariah Carey and Seal CDs. The live performance of the Indian drum she saw as the party's climax.

Four couples from the Tropicana arrived well dressed in sports clothes. Ralph Paskevich was the Folies stage manager. His wife, Tracey, was a secretary in the executive office of another casino. They were about ten years older than Sue and Debbie, but had been friends since the girls joined the show. Gary Meadows and his wife, Carol, were also in their late-30's. Gary had one of the singing leads in the Folies. Carol worked as the wardrobe manager for Starlight Express, the big production show at the Hilton. Sam Pullman and his wife, Alice, were middle-aged. He was a craps pit boss. Alice had a real estate license, but she considered herself retired. The fourth couple was not married, but bar manager Bobby Cling had lived with Ginger, a cocktail waitress, so long that none of their friends could remember her last name.

From the entrepreneurial side of their lives, Debbie had invited Sid Bacall, their Laundromat partner; Maxine Kellerman, their beauty parlor partner; and Ron and Betty Solomon, their real estate partners. With Ramon and his uncle, the party was an even sixteen. The number was about the comfortable limit for a party that extended across the space of the living room-dining room area onto the rear patio.

Debbie and Sue had acquaintances their own age, but they seldom, if ever, invited them into their homes. With the exception of Ramon and his uncle, the friendships of the other guests had been tested over five or six years. For the girls, these trusted friends seemed like family.

The girls could have had dates for the party, but the men they might have invited would have been a bothersome inconvenience. They considered no prospects worthy of inclusion. What little home and family time they had was sacrosanct.

When Anglo brought in the steaming stack of corn from the patio, Debbie called the guests around the buffet table.

"Being a Southern girl," Debbie announced, "I feel like we need a grace said over this beautiful food. I have been told by Ramon that among the Indians of his tribe, Booker is considered a holy man. So since he is the nearest thing we have to a priest, I'd like to ask him to say the grace."

Anglo was surprised by the request, but as all eyes were on him, he closed his eyes and bowed his head.

"Blessed are we by Mother Earth and Father Sky to have such a feast laid before us. We accept these gifts in honor of the Creator who made us all that we should celebrate life and live in peace together. Amen."

Debbie, Ron Solomon, and Sam Pullman echoed the amen, and soon the room was filled with the happy noise of people circling the table, filling their plates with food and making conversational praise for each dish. Debbie's North Carolina barbecue pork, pulled from a slow-cooked shoulder and flavored with a pungent vinegar-tomato-spice sauce, drew special praise, as did Booker's Indian corn which he dehusked tableside. Conversational groups before the meal became supper groups, whose members balanced their plates on their laps and ate with enthusiasm.

Anglo especially enjoyed Maxine's spinach casserole, and a layered eggplant dish prepared by Tracey Paskevich. Betty Solomon had baked three loaves of plaited egg bread that was soft, chewy and irresistible. Sue had baked two chocolate layer cakes for dessert.

"It's not a real feast for me," Sue said as she served, "unless we finish with my grandmother's chocolate cake. Believe it or not, I made them from scratch. If this isn't love, I don't know what is."

After the large meal, the guests lounged in the living room like contented bears. There were not enough seats on the sofa and upholstered chairs, so some used throw pillows to sit on the carpet and leaned against whoever or whatever was available. The music and the lights were soft. The need for conversation was minimal.

In the kitchen, Sue was helping Debbie scrape plates for the dishwasher when Maxine came in to whisper.

"The uncle is a very good looking man. Why didn't you tell me?"

"I didn't know that you were looking," Sue responded.

"Honey," Maxine said, "I'm always looking. I may be 40, divorced, and broad in the hips, but I'm not out of the game yet."

"Go for it," Sue encouraged. "He's not my date."

"You know what I have a mad desire to do?" Maxine asked.

"Tell us," Debbie said, suppressing a giggle.

"I want to braid the man's hair. You know, Indian style. I'd part his hair right down the middle and give him two of the tightest braids he ever had. Let 'em drape behind the ears and fall over his shoulders down his chest."

"Stop it," Debbie teased. "You're making me hot."

"Funny," Maxine said with sarcasm.

"Look," Sue advised, "I'm not afraid to approach him. We're all family here. He might like to have his hair done before we ask him to sing."

"I dare you," Debbie said.

"Do it," Maxine encouraged.

"You two are the oldest teenagers in Las Vegas, I swear."

Sue went into the living room where Anglo sat on the floor, relaxing in the company of the others.

"Uncle Booker," Sue began, "while we are sitting around digesting our supper, would you like to have your hair braided? Maxine is a beautician, and she would love to do it."

Anglo smiled, thinking how unpredictable young women can be.

"At the pueblo, I have a tribal sister who braids my hair. It is a very generous thing to do, and something that I have missed. I would be very pleased to have Maxine braid my hair. It will be my meditation for the drum."

Maxine soon appeared with a straight back chair from the dining room and the comb and brush of her trade. Anglo took his place in the chair, sitting very erect with his elbows bent and his hands placed palm down on his thighs. He closed his eyes as Maxine began to comb his long hair and make the part in preparation for braiding. His breathing gradually became almost imperceptible. From across the room he appeared as motionless as a man sculpted out of wood by an artful hand that had formed the face into the gentlest of expressions.

The onlookers seemed fascinated by the braiding ritual. Carol Meadows left her place on the floor to stand behind Maxine so she

could see the work more closely. Gary Meadows
ran his hand through his own hair, imagining
what emotional warmth the braiding must generate. Sam Pullman felt his own balding scalp and
thin hair and resigned himself to foregoing the
braids. Nevertheless, he vicariously enjoyed the
experience being enacted before him. There was
something soothing, even in the watching.

Dancer had never experienced the intimacy of
white society. His casino dates and restaurant
dinners had not prepared him for the evocative
friendships he was witness to this night. There
was a warmth and generosity of spirit here that
he had not anticipated, not thought possible in
white culture. These people, this feast, was not
unlike a gathering of his own kind.

Now Maxine, who had first cut and styled
his hair, was making an intimate gift to Anglo,
who accepted it as though she was his clan
sister. How could strangers come into such
quick relationships? It was very confusing to
Dancer.

An hour passed in quiet comfort as Maxine
worked meticulously on Anglo's hair while the
others watched or engaged in muted conversations. Debbie had not noticed that the final CD
in her program had ended, and that the only
background sound was the purr of the air-conditioning. At a less mature party, she would have
felt the need to enliven the moment with loud
music or the presentation of a group participation

game, but her own satisfaction level did not pro-
voke it.

Maxine completed the braiding by positioning
the two locks of hair over Anglo's shoulders. Then
she stood in front of him to admire her work.

"You look like you ought to be on the face
of a nickel," she said to Booker.

Anglo opened his eyes and looked up into her
face. "I believe that I already am."

She looked perplexed until he grinned and
gave her a wink of his right eye. Maxine smiled
broadly as she recognized the sincerity of the
compliment. Impulsively, she kissed him on his
cheek.

"You have made one cheek very happy and
the other cheek very jealous," Anglo said.

Maxine laughed and kissed his other cheek. In
response, Anglo kissed her on each cheek.

The exchange was observed by everyone in
the room, but Debbie made the first aside.

"What is going on here, Maxine? Are you trying to turn this into a make-out party?"

Maxine actually blushed, but accepted the good
humor and attention of her friends with an
aroused comeback.

"In case you didn't know," she posed theatri-
cally, "this is the way we thank each other in
the upper class."

The remark made everyone laugh, but Maxine
regretted that the spell of her connection with
Anglo was broken.

"Now that we are wide awake," Debbie cajoled her sedate guests, "I think it is time to ask Uncle Booker and Ramon to sing for us."

The applause was Sue's cue to hand Anglo his drum and beater and to coax Ramon to come to the front of the room and stand beside him. The other guests rearranged themselves to give their attention to the performers.

"I first heard Pueblo songs," Anglo began, "when I was harvesting mesquite wood in the desert plains around Santa Fe. The father and son whom I was helping occasionally sang as they worked. Although I did not know the meaning of the words or even understand the music, I sensed something profound. Later, as I came to hear the drum with the singing, I realized that in ceremony or in everyday acts, the songs are a form of worship. This is so because Native American peoples do not separate life into spiritual and secular segments. Their religion is the way they live their lives.

"Ramon and I have never sung together before, but he knows all the songs of his people. I know only a few. There are thousands, and more are being written every day. The head singer of a drum group can hear a song one time and teach it to his own drum the next day. I am not that skilled, although I will serve as the head singer tonight.

"I will start the drumbeat and sing the first line of the song. Ramon will know the song and sing it with me as I repeat the line. Then we will sing the song through and keep repeating it over and over until I give Ramon a drum cue that the next time will be the last time through.

"We will sing about the raising of the sun. We will sing an Honor Song to thank our host. We will sing a friendship song and a song to bless the harvest season. The words to these songs are simple. They are not essential to understanding. Neither is the skill of the singers. Do not try to think or to analyze. Be one with the drum and understanding will come."

The drumbeat began slowly, its sound reverberating in the room in steady, equal waves. It surrounded and penetrated the guests. They were unaccustomed to an intensity which did not assume loudness. Then Anglo began the song. He startled them. His voice was full-throated, even strained. The notes seemed off-key, the words foreign, unlike any language that they knew. Before they could adjust, Dancer added his voice in the same full measure. There was no harmony. The voices were in close unison singing a complex pattern against the solid rhythm of the drum. Many of the guests looked to each other for confirmation of their confusion. They had no cultural reference by which to know if the men sang well or not.

The singers did not interact. Their eyes were closed. Their total focus was the song. The minds of the guests, however, were adrift in a sea of comparisons. Bobby Cling smiled, thinking of old western movies where Indians went on the warpath with such songs. Gary Meadows was puzzled by the complexity of the sounds, which he could not picture noted on sheet music. He was not confident, even with his degree in vocal performance, that he could sing them.

Alice Pullman, who had an extensive record collection of Broadway musicals, wondered how long she could stand to listen to the incoherent hollering. Sid Bacall was of much the same opinion, although his musical taste was confined to classic rock and roll. Ron and Betty Solomon struggled to be politely correct by tapping their feet in time with the drum. Carol Meadows kept time, too, but wondered how much more effective the performance might have been if the men had dressed in tribal regalia.

Maxine Kellerman wanted to like the music because of her attraction to Anglo, but even in her fantasy she could not see herself going to a powwow or responding to Indian culture. The music was a disappointing turn-off for her. She was embarrassed by it, and was concerned about what she could say to Booker after the performance.

Sam Pullman, Tracey Pashevick, and Ginger, whose last name had been forgotten, had sufficient curiosity to be entertained by the singers. They did not understand the songs, but, like opera, they could appreciate it for what it was—a vocal fireworks.

Sue, especially, and Debbie, perhaps less so—because of their previous experience with Anglo at Red Rock Canyon—were enraptured by the performance. Their attention was total, and they experienced an indefinable uplift that seemed concentrated in the right sides of their chests. Ralph Paskevich was similarly affected, and he didn't know why. The drum had discovered a resonant place in him that connected him to the circle of the singers. All Ralph understood was that the feeling was good.

Anglo had not paused long enough for applause between songs. The drum was still resonating from the previous song when the next began. For most people in the room, they could not distinguish one song from the next. The end was unanticipated. The cue came with the opening of the singers' eyes.

The applause was polite and uneven according to the various levels of satisfaction. Guests without positive comments sought excuse by rushing off to the bathrooms. Debbie served another round of coffee; casserole dishes and serving platters were recovered by the cooks; and couple by couple, the guests embraced farewells and went out into the warm midnight.

CHAPTER TWENTY-SIX

The fall in Las Vegas is like a milder summer with average highs and lows twenty degrees more temperate. Since the air is still dry, an 80-degree day can seem almost refreshing after the scorching period. Daybreak temperatures in the low 50's can feel chilly.

Anglo and Dancer worked their day-for-night schedules, but Anglo was no longer excluded from the company of his host and his two associates. On the nights that he did not have a date, Dancer continued to look for Anglo as a meal companion. Once, sometimes twice a week, they were joined by one or both girls. Sue and Debbie were curious about Uncle Booker's background, and they wanted more details than Ramon was able to provide from native rumors.

Dancer felt a cultural taboo against asking direct personal questions that was not shared by the showgirls. Locked together in a restaurant booth, the women seemed shameless in their questioning of Anglo. Dancer might have winced at their prying if he had permitted himself to display emotion, but he remained reserved. He realized that he, too, wanted to know how such a man as Anglo came to be.

As far as the girls were concerned, Uncle Booker was hard to draw out. Given the type of interest that they were expressing in his life, most men in their experience would have taken center stage for a lengthy life-story soliloquy. Anglo responded to their questions, but he did not elaborate on the answers. The girls found his responses maddening, but it only exacerbated their desire to know more.

"What did you do in Norfolk?" Sue asked as a follow-up question.

"I worked in real estate," Anglo replied.

"Were you married?"

"Yes."

"Any children?"

"Yes, a son and a daughter."

"Where are they now?"

"In Norfolk and Virginia Beach."

"Are you divorced?" Debbie pursued.

"Yes."

"Do you see them?" Sue continued.

"I haven't seen them in almost a year," Anglo said gently.

"Do they know that you live with the Indians?" Debbie asked.

"Yes, they know."

"Maybe they will come for a visit," Sue suggested.

"Yes," Anglo smiled. "That would be good."

Piece by piece, over a period of three weeks of casual dinners together, the girls satisfied themselves on the framework of the Winn Conover—Booker Jones—Anglo-of-the-Indians transition. The question of why he had radically changed his life was less structured for them.

"You had everything most people want," Sue observed. "Why did you walk away from it?"

"There was no happiness in it," Anglo said simply.

"If that is not happy," Debbie added, "what is?"

"Happiness is not inherent in things," Anglo responded. "Happiness is our natural state when we realize our connection to Creation."

"How do you do that?" Sue asked sincerely.

"Be silent. Look within. Ask the question 'Who am I?' and follow the 'I' thought to the center of Reality."

"Just like that?" Debbie challenged.

"Just like that," Anglo affirmed. "I myself came to it by desperation, even by accident. It is very difficult to watch your every thought, but if you do, you can slow thought down to nothingness. That is when you see the Truth about happiness."

"What does this have to do with living with Indians?" Sue asked.

Anglo laughed at the inadequacy of words. "Traditional Indians still live very close to Creation, to what we call Nature. They attune themselves to the Power behind Creation. They experience it in all natural forms which they identify as spirits. Their door to Reality seems very open to me. I feel comfortable in their lifestyle because of its connection to spirit. I love them for their sacrifice and dedication."

The girls didn't know how to respond. They looked at Ramon, but he offered no clue as to what he was thinking. To fill a silence that they felt was awkward, Debbie changed the subject.

"Let's order the biggest, chocolatiest, most outrageous dessert in the house. I've got a bunch of sins to confess this week. One more won't make any difference."

"I was raised a Baptist," Sue responded lightly. "It's not that easy for me."

"What do you do with your sins?" Debbie asked Anglo half-jokingly.

"There is only one sin," he said, looking into their faces. "Separation from our Source. All error begins in that moment and takes unnumbered forms."

"Whoa," Debbie reacted. "That's too heavy for me. Let's get back to choosing a dessert."

Back at Dancer's apartment, the two men sat on the veranda to await sunrise. Anglo offered the pipe to the six directions, filled and lit it, smoked a few puffs and then passed it to Dancer. They had not spoken since their goodbyes to the girls in front of the restaurant.

"This is not your place, is it?" Dancer asked.

"It is not Red Rock Canyon," Anglo admitted.

"Then why do you stay? Your home is on the pueblo."

"I am seeking a vision."

"And you think that I am to play a part?"

"Yes."

"You will find no spirit guides in the stock-room caves of the Tropicana," Dancer chided. "You need a cacique and a holy place."

"I know a place," Anglo said.

"Where?"

"The Valley of Fire."

"How do you know this place?"

"Carlos and I made prayers there and left gifts."

"On what day?" Dancer asked in disbelief.

"On the dawn after we first saw you."

Dancer was quiet for some minutes and allowed the pipe to go out in his hand. He passed it back to Anglo to be relit.

"If you must make your vision quest here, I will help you. We must make preparations. How many days do you need?"

"What would you do?" Anglo asked.

"Four days is traditional. I would do no less than three after four days of fasting and purification. You have to reduce your water intake gradually so that you can stand the thirst. It would be a mistake to gorge water before you go up on the hill. It also shows lack of faith."

"I understand," Anglo acknowledged.

"I will fast and purify with you, and I will make the tobacco ties to form the sacred circle. I will get the red willow bark, the cloth, and the string. We will need the pipe and the eagle feathers. I will make the other items as my gift to you."

"I am grateful."

"I know the ceremony, but I am no priest," Dancer cautioned.

"All is as it should be," Anglo replied.

"Do not do this thing lightly," Dancer warned. "And do not let pride keep you on the hill until you die. It is no dishonor to come down."

"I understand."

"What could I tell the police if I had to carry down your dead body?"

"I understand your concerns."

"I hate to involve Sue and Debbie, but we may need some backup if we have to hike in. We need to find a remote spot so the ceremony won't be interrupted, but it is traditional that family be nearby to restore us to life at the end."

"Let's ask them to support us," Anglo agreed.

"All this is very—" Dancer could not find the word.

"Unorthodox," Anglo said.

"Yes, strange." Dancer thought for a few moments. "I will have to take my vacation week from the Folies. When do you want to begin?"

"As soon as you can get free."

"I'll ask tomorrow."

"Good," Anglo said. "When you have the dates, I will give notice at my job."

CHAPTER TWENTY-SEVEN

Dancer had to wait three weeks before his vacation began. It was time enough to make the preparations, but there were many details to work out. The task gave a new meaning and purpose to his daily life, and he seemed energized by it.

It would take at least two trips into the Valley of Fire to find and prepare the vision quest site. When the site was selected, the area would have to be cleaned and a shelter built. The most practical shelter, given the remoteness of the envisioned area, would be a pit covered by a lean-to. They would have to carry the tools and building materials in on their backs. Dancer hoped to locate enough sage along the entry route to cut on the day of the quest. The area would also have to be scouted for other needed natural resources.

A recurring discussion was on what to do about the sweatbath, the prayer and purifying ritual usually begun at sunset so that it was dark when the quester reached the hill. It was decided that they would carry in enough poles to make a miniature tipi, just large enough for two men, and dig a pit for the stones. The seven round stones would have to be found in a nearby arroyo, where they might also find enough firewood—driven downstream in the summer floods—to heat the stones. The poles, they decided, could then be used to construct the helper's shelter.

The helper, Dancer, would wait out of sight below the hill while Anglo faced his ordeal. He could eat and drink and warm himself with a fire if needed. He would be expected to pray for his friend, and have water and food ready when the quest was done, but his primary job was waiting.

Dancer did not discuss his fears with Anglo. First, there was the weather, which was unpredictable in late September. It could be very hot during the day and chilly at night. There was always the possibility of thunderstorms, which could be especially violent when the northern cold fronts from Canada reached across the mountains and collided with the desert heat stored from summer. There could be lightning strikes and sheets of driving rain. Anglo, exposed on the hill, would be severely tested not only by the storm, but by the abundant water that he could not drink.

A second fear arose from snakes and poisonous insects. Dancer would carefully clean and inspect the area around the vision circle, but once the pit was dug and shaded by the lean-to, it might attract a speckled rattlesnake or scorpions. It was a rule when sleeping in the desert to awake slowly, carefully. Do not alarm the snake or scorpion who has also shared the dark warmth of your blanket. Always shake out your moccasins for the scorpions sleeping there. Dancer knew the stories of vision questers who had been bitten or stung within the circle, and seeing it as a further test, had remained on the hill. Some lived to become tribal legends. Most were found dead. What would Anglo do? Dancer would not speculate.

The two men altered their sleeping schedules to have more daytime hours for gathering necessary supplies. They purchased canvas and a second-hand quilt for the portable sweatlodge. At a military surplus store they picked up two entrenching tools, small collapsible shovels, a lightweight camouflaged tarp in Desert Storm colors for the lean-to cover, and some sturdy aluminum tent poles that could be assembled in sections. Since they could not depend on finding pole-length wood in the desert, they bought enough poles for both the sweatlodge and the lean-to. Once Anglo was on the hill, Dancer planned to dismantle the sweatlodge and use the poles and canvas to erect a more convenient shelter. The plan was to backpack all of the building materials into the site and cache them, rolled up, in the waterproof camouflaged tarp. Then on the final trip, their loads would contain ceremonial items and normal camping supplies.

"We'd better cache some extra canteens of water on the first trips," Anglo suggested. "We'll need them for the sweat and the wash-down before going up on the hill."

It is not the way of Native American peoples to ask favors. It is the responsibility of neighbors to anticipate the needs of their friends and to do what is needed without negotiation or thought of quid pro quo. Dancer was uncertain how to approach Debbie and Sue for their support, although he needed them to provide transportation to the Valley of Fire and to back up the men if Anglo became ill.

Dancer would not trust the park officials. He would not apply for a camping permit or tell them where he was going and when. Federal and state park officials had a reputation for sabotaging Indian ceremonies. Indian gatherings had even been outlawed on park lands in recent history. In places where ceremonies had been held for centuries, Indians were not allowed their sacred rites. Their modern lawyers failed to preserve the traditional grounds even when they filed suits for the freedom of religion. The white man's right to picnic superseded all spiritual claims.

So Dancer and Anglo would have to sneak into the holy land and conduct the most important ceremony of their lives in secret. And for safety and security, Dancer would trust, and bring himself to ask the help of, two young white women who could never comprehend the importance of their duty.

"Will you stop beating around the bush," Debbie complained to Dancer. "If you want us to drive you guys to a campsite, just ask."

"Actually," Anglo clarified, "we need to make three trips to the Valley of Fire. One to find a place, a little day trip. One to bring in supplies and prepare the site, maybe an overnight trip. And finally, we need to be dropped off and picked up five days later."

"Why don't you ask for the moon and the stars?" Debbie asked. "What do you think we are? Den mothers for boy scouts?"

"We'd be glad to help," Sue said with finality. "Why don't we make the first trip a picnic. I've never seen the Valley of Fire."

"I'll make the sandwiches," Debbie said quickly.

"Then what was all that sarcasm about?" Sue demanded.

"I was just giving them a hard time," Debbie defended. "I don't want people to think I'm easy."

On the first trip to Valley of Fire State Park, the foursome in the BMW might have been tourists had they not entered the park at sunrise. Their first stop was on the loop road to Atlatl Rock. Anglo followed Dancer away from the visitor trek for about twenty minutes into the wilderness. Dancer pointed out potential campsites and explored the crowns of sandstone, but was not satisfied that he had found the appropriate quest site.

Next Sue followed another loop road near the location of the petrified logs. Dancer returned to the car after less than ten minutes of reconnaissance. "Too much people," was his only comment.

Anglo referred to his Valley of Fire picture book and directed Sue to Petroglyph Canyon, where he led the other three on a walking tour to Mouse's Tank.

Dancer was struck by the petroglyphs and paused beneath them to squat on the ground in reflection.

"This is a holy place," he whispered to Anglo as they passed through the narrows of the walled canyon.

"I know," Anglo agreed. "This is the place where Carlos and I made our prayers and left our gifts."

The girls complained about walking in the deep sand and the distance to Mouse's Tank, but Anglo's narrative and the geological wonder of the place itself kept them entertained.

"Too bad this canyon is so popular with tourists," Anglo said to Dancer.

Dancer nodded. "This place has been violated for 100 years and still it has power. Many visions were revealed here, but it is no longer quiet enough. There are too many voices now."

The girls required refreshment when they returned

to the parking area, so they made an early morning meal.

"I hope that you can find something by noon," Debbie said. "I'd like to avoid the heat if we can."

The end of the road past Petroglyph Canyon was Rainbow Vista, which was the trailhead for hiking trails to Fire Canyon and Silica Dome and a much longer trail to the White Domes area. Dancer wanted to explore the four-mile trail to the White Domes which lay across a remote section of the park. Sue and Debbie left the men with a canteen of water and retreated to the air-conditioned comfort of the Visitor Center where they could peruse the exhibits.

"Do not mention that we are looking for a campsite," Dancer instructed the women. "We want to camp in private."

"No problem," Debbie assured him. "We'll come back for you in a couple of hours."

Anglo followed Dancer along the trail for a mile. The terrain was rugged and difficult to cross in each direction. Dancer seemed to be looking for something when he left the trail. Anglo kept pace with him around sandstone boulders and across parched, open areas until they came to a desert wash which Dancer followed. A lone, rare cottonwood tree, stunted and rising out of the sand floor, indicated water deep below the surface. Anglo had lost his sense of direction, but he trusted Dancer to find their way back to the trail. They were perhaps two miles or more into the wilderness when Dancer stopped.

"This is a good place," he explained. "No one will see the campfire. No one has walked this way for many moons."

The men smiled at the reference to Indian time.

"We can make a camp along this wash and select a hill beyond the big boulders towards the gray mountains. How does this place feel to you?"

Anglo walked in a circle to view all aspects of the area. "Let us choose a hill," he said in confirmation.

The hill that they selected was a natural mound of sand tufted sparsely with brush. It stood alone and exposed. Its virtue was that a pit could be dug into its crown, which was broad enough to accommodate the 15-foot circle of tobacco ties. The men marked the hill with rocks that they collected and carefully stacked in a circle. Anglo buried a small tie of red willow bark and one of cornmeal at the center of the stones as an offering, and then the men sat cross-legged on the hill and prayed.

While leaving the area, Dancer carefully covered the evidence of their visit by brushing away their tracks as they withdrew. When their back-trail made a turn, Dancer carefully arranged rocks as a marker that only he and Anglo could read.

To any other observer, the arrangement seemed randomly natural. To them, the marker indicated direction and distance. Finally they broke clear of the rock formations and could see the White Domes trail. A final marker was made just off the trail, and they returned to the trailhead where the girls were waiting.

A week later, Dancer used his night off for the second trip. The girls drove the men into the park at first light and unloaded their gear and supplies at the White Domes trailhead. In addition to the two bundles of canvas and tarp tied up to be carried on their backs, the men also had to carry six canteens of water and personal haversacks containing food and small items needed for their work. They had about 33 hours to prepare the site and get back to the trailhead, where Sue would pick them up at 3 p.m. the following day.

"Who has a watch?" Sue inquired.

Both men shook their heads in the negative and held up their hands to reveal naked wrists.

"How will you know the time?" she demanded. "I don't want to be sitting here in the sun waiting for you."

"The sun will tell us," Dancer assured her. "It's a pretty good clock."

"What if it rains?"

"Then we will be wet when you come back," Dancer said as a joke.

"If you are not here, how long should I wait

before I call the Park Rangers?" Sue said in earnest.

"Come back two days at the same hour and wait for an hour. If we are not here the third time, don't bother to call the Rangers, call a priest because we will be dead."

"Don't say things like that," Sue insisted. "Just be here."

"This is my home," Dancer said with an expanse of his arms. "What have I to fear here?"

When they reached the area of the hill, they found a rocky outcrop above the dry gully they had previously followed and made their camp. The ropes supporting the heavy packs had dug into their shoulders, and they were glad to put the packs down. The walk in had taken nearly two hours because Dancer had made two false exits off the main trail, and then had erased all signs of their passage from the false exits to the real exit and beyond a hundred yards into the rocks. Anglo, who had learned trail-covering skills for his passage to Nita's secret grave on a forested mountain, learned new skills by watching Dancer work.

While the morning was still relatively cool, Dancer suggested that they clear the hill, dig the pit, and cover it with the sectioned poles and camouflaged tarp. The rocks that previously identified the hill could be used to keep the edges of the covering secure. It took some time to complete the project, the hole being about six feet long, three feet wide, and four feet deep. The two men welcomed the shade of their rocky encampment, where they took water and ate a simple meal of dried fruit and cold refried beans wrapped in soft tortillas.

The afternoon sun was hot, but with broad-brimmed straw hats and long-sleeved shirts, they were comfortable collecting the pale gray driftwood along the arroyo. It took half an hour to find an armload of firewood, and it would take many armloads to build a square stack of interlocking pieces high enough to heat the seven double-fist-sized stones for the sweatlodge. Finding the right stones was not easy. Dancer inspected the prospective stones carefully, even smelling them before he cracked them together to test their solidarity. Finally seven were selected and wrapped in the quilt to be hidden in their cache.

Anglo asked why Dancer had smelled the rocks while selecting them.

"If a coyote made pee on the stone, you would smell him in the sweatlodge as soon as the water hit it. You would smell it like he had peed on your head."

Anglo chuckled at the thought, and Dancer joined him, his face forming a laugh, his lips open and his breath coming out in staccato, but without sound.

When the sun began to set, the men settled into their campsite and laid out their blanket beds on the soft sand floor of the wash. Dancer had placed sticks for a campfire between them, but they did not light them until very late. They wanted nothing to steal the lights from the sky. The shadows of evening merged together into twilight, and each man eagerly awaited the evening star, a dependable friend who preceded the coming of the moon. The star was a peaceful reassurance of day yielding to night. The evening star had spoken to poets of every culture and every generation. It had been the subject of countless Indian love songs played on hand-made cedar flutes.

The majestic moon made ascending entry onto the stage of the sky, gliding up an unseen stair with awe-evoking grace. The moon was near harvest full, but whatever its phase, it was never considered indelicate or unbalanced. In the dry, clear desert sky, the moon seemed gigantic as it first appeared over the crags of mountaintops. It rose steadily, even quickly, with such luminescence that light itself might have been named after it. And thus were Anglo and Dancer moonstruck into silence and ancient wonder. The moon could be a vehicle to ride or a light to pour the self into. Its character had nothing to do with science. The coyotes began their howling calls across the desert. What were they saying about the moon?

The Earth turned, and the sunrise revealed two men sitting on a sand mound in a desert wilderness. They faced the East, and from their position they observed a coyote, two blacktail jackrabbits, and several kangaroo rats en route to their daytime hideaways. The air was chilled and the men were wrapped in blankets. The stillness of the morning and their own lack of movement made them appear like the red sandstone outcroppings around them, which the wind and rain had carved into statuary. All across the Southwest, traditional Indians also waited in reverence to greet the sun. In these moments they were connected in spirit. Perhaps by these bonds, they held the Earth together.

CHAPTER TWENTY-EIGHT

Before leaving the campsite, Anglo and Dancer climbed up on a ledge under the protective overhead outcrop and found two large niches in the rock in which to cache their retied bundles. Each made a broom of sagebrush and worked to remove signs of their encampment. Dancer buried the remnants of the campfire, and then they backed out of the area, carefully sweeping their tracks behind them and walking on rocks wherever possible. When they came across tracks made by animals or lizards in the night, they crossed them without disturbing the lines of the creatures' travels.

They reached the trailhead before the agreed hour and found a place off the road to wait in the shade of a boulder mass. The only things that they had carried out were their haversacks and a single canteen which still contained water. They had accomplished all their work on this single supply. The other five canteens remained full and hidden in the cache.

They could see the dust raised by Sue's car

before they saw the vehicle itself. Sue stopped at the end of the road, and they could see her craning her neck in an effort to find them. The digging on the hill, and the climbing in the red powder dust of the sandstone had coated their clothing and hats, and put a patina on their exposed hands and faces so that they resembled the rocks themselves. Sue did not see them until they moved out of the shadows of the rocks. They startled her. Her first impression was that they had materialized beside the road as if beamed to earth by a starship.

As they approached the car, she got out to inspect them.

"Don't you two look a sight! If it wasn't for the openings around your eyes you could hardly pass for human. You look like coal miners coming up from the mines. Only the color is different. I'll bet you could use a cold drink. I brought a cooler-full."

Sue insisted that the men dust themselves off before she would allow them into her car. She did most of the talking on the drive back to Las Vegas.

"Well, next week is the big one. I can't imagine what you two will look like after five days. Debbie and I are going to bring the video camera for that one."

Dancer accepted no dates and drank no alcohol in the days preceding the final trip to the Valley of Fire. He took his responsibility to

Anglo seriously and kept the same gradual fasting habits as his uncle. In the last days, they would eat only fruit and completely empty their bowels. Their rations of water were gradually reduced as well. The object was to condition the body to less and to obviate the need to defecate, or even urinate, during the confinement on the hill. If the need to urinate arose, it was permissible to stand at the edge of the circle and direct the stream outside it.

Dancer spent most of his free time preparing the ceremonial items. Over 400 tobacco ties would be needed to outline the sacred circle. Dancer used a mixture of willow bark and Bull Durham tobacco tied into two-inch squares of colored broadcloth. Two colors were alternated and the small pouches tied about two inches apart on a long, medium-weight cotton kite string. The product of the labor was wrapped around a roll of felt flags Dancer had made and adorned with painted symbols and put into the top of a backpack partially filled with fresh sage leaves collected by local Indians near Mt. Charleston. Dancer had found this source for fresh sage after he discovered it was not abundant on the route to the hill.

All the ceremonial elements were prepared and packed. Dancer and Anglo appeared to be normal during the last days at their jobs, but they were far removed from the routine activity. Their minds were very quiet. They watched the behavior of Ramon Ortiz and Booker Jones from places in the hearts of their being where Dancer and Anglo dwelled. The gradual fasting that had been going on for weeks, and was now reduced to small amounts of fruit and water, would have sapped the strength and mental abilities of persons focused on the physical body. But Dancer and Anglo felt well and fit, and the level of their awareness was a metaphor for the All-Seeing-Eye, that which represents all-pervading intelligence. The peace that they felt was a Reality that required no judgment. They had stopped talking about the preparations and about the things to be done when they returned to the area of the hill. There was no more need of talk. Even their prayers were wordless. Being itself was the purest form of their worship.

So even when Ramon appeared on stage in his compromised regalia and danced against the background of bare-breasted showgirls, he was sanctified. And Anglo, cleaning out the foul kitchen grease pit—a job considered punishment—was untroubled, untouched by doing work others refused to do. It did not matter what the body was doing as long as the man inside was consecrated.

The religions of the world celebrate their saints as selfless individuals, but they do not understand the path human beings must walk to achieve such awareness. The metaphor of nature is predominant in the experience of saints. They venture alone to mountaintops. They risk their lives in the wilderness. They go into the desert. They sit beside the still waters. These are the natural places that restore their souls.

Sue and Debbie speculated about the purpose of the men's camping trip. They suspected that there was something ritualistic about it, but they were afraid to probe for answers. They had first concluded that Ramon was helping Booker to perform some Indian thing, but as the event neared, they sensed that he was intensely involved too.

"They are being awfully quiet," Debbie noted. "There is something serious going on."

"Maybe they are going to steal horses and go on the warpath," Sue said in jest.

"If they want scalps," Debbie offered, "I've got a closet full of wigs."

"We can laugh, but being an Indian in our world can't be fun for them," Sue said. "You should have seen Ramon when I dropped the guys off in the park. He came alive. All I could see was rocks and sand and hardship. He saw it as home."

"Those guys don't require much, do they?" Debbie noted sincerely.

"They really don't."

"Maybe they are happier than we are," Debbie said. "We are working our plan here every day in order to get someplace else. I wonder if we will be completely happy when we get there? The price is too high if we're not. And then it is too late."

"Happiness is not cheap. You have got to work for it," Sue reminded her friend.

"Why?" Debbie asked in defiance.

"Because that's the way it is."

"Well, it's not fair. It's too hard. It costs too much."

"So plan on a smaller house, a cheaper car, one kid instead of two. Reduce your expectations," Sue advised.

"It's always about things, isn't it?" Debbie said in despair. "Our happiness always seems dependent on things. It is always in the future. But I want to be happy now."

"Well, what's your problem? You have a nice house, a new car, an investment portfolio, a good job. You've got your health. You're beautiful. What the hell is stopping you?"

"The same thing that is stopping you," Debbie challenged, pointing her finger at Sue. "And it has nothing to do with men, or marriage."

Sue started to respond, but then lowered the arm that had started to gesture and was silent. Finally, she crossed the room to her friend and quietly said, "I guess we have everything, and we have nothing. Ain't life a bitch?"

CHAPTER TWENTY-NINE

The late afternoon drive to Valley of Fire State Park was made mostly in silence. For once, Sue did not automatically punch on her CD player. Sue and Debbie had their speculations confirmed about the seriousness of the trip when they saw the countenances of the men. They had lost weight, that was evident, but it was their faces which caused their restraint. Booker smiled in response to their greeting, and Ramon loaded the trunk of the car, but the focus in their eyes was on something far away.

The girls were used to having conversations with Ramon in which he never looked directly into their faces. They had come to accept this, and his reluctance to be talkative, as cultural eccentricities. Recently, however, his strangeness—and that of his uncle—had risen to another level.

Sue had later tried to articulate it to Debbie. "It's like they are somewhere else until you cause them to respond to you. They are on channel four while we are watching channel twelve. But if we press the remote, they will click back into our lives. Then you have their attention. They are good listeners. But if you don't require them to be here, they aren't."

When they reached the trailhead and unloaded the car, the girls felt compelled to kiss each man on the cheek and wish him well. It was their way of conveying a blessing, but their sentiments were shadowed by an unnamed apprehension. They watched the men until the trail took them out of sight.

"Why didn't you ask them?" Debbie said in complaint. "This is not just a camping trip, and we both know it."

"Why didn't you ask?"

"Because it seemed so private to them," Debbie said in defense.

"Do you know what you call that?" Sue asked with a smile that showed her pride. Debbie nodded for an answer. "You call that respect."

Without prompting, Dancer and Anglo worked as a team to cover their tracks along the White Domes trail. When they came to their exit marker, they backed their way across the sand into the rocks with expert moves, not allowing any displaced twig or broken insect trail to betray their passage. They moved quickly and silently over the familiar landscape, observing their trail markers as friendly signs directing them to their goal. The way was unmarred by evidence of any other human travel or occupation. They had expected none, but the ground nevertheless received their intense scrutiny. Finally they entered the dry wash and followed it to the site of their previous camp, with its high rock niches which held their cache.

There was no need to rush. During the remaining hours of daylight they would check the hill, making sure that their work there had not been discovered. They were into the last day of their mutual fast so there was no meal to prepare. The final night before the ordeal was reserved for contemplation and prayer. There was still time to call off the ceremony. There was no shame attached to the admission of not being ready.

After the sunrise welcome ritual, the men would dig the pit for the hot stones and erect the sweatlodge. The poles would be set as a frame for the tipi and then covered by the quilt, which might have to be tied into place. A flap would be left for entry. Then the canvas covering would be made fast over the quilt and sand piled around its edges to make sure no light entered. The door flap would be aligned to the East, the firepit dug, and the wood stacked in cross-hatched layers about twelve feet from the opening. The seven stones would be arranged carefully at the center of the woodpile so that they would be fired on all sides. The final preparations would be checking the closed sweatlodge for complete darkness and spreading the inside ground with sage. The canteens would be placed beside the tipi when they were needed.

Next, the men would go to the hill and erect the lean-to over the hole they had previously dug. The poles and tarp which had concealed the dig would now be employed to construct the shelter. The open end of the lean-to would occupy one quadrant of the holy circle facing East. Its position would allow for free movement in the other three quarters of the circle. By tradition, the man in the circle would be naked except for his sleeping blanket. His only other protection from the sun and the weather would be his sheltered hole.

Dancer would next place the ceremonial flags and once again explain their symbology to Anglo. It was important that the vision quester accept the power of the flags to protect him from evil, and at the same time realize that they also summoned the spirit world. Finally, Dancer would spread sage leaves on the ground and then form the sacred circle by carefully laying the string of tobacco ties around its perimeter. Then no one but the vision quester could enter the circle. An end of the tie would be lifted like a door for the man to enter, and then it would be replaced to close the circle as a seal not to be broken. Here, naked and alone, a man offers himself to his Creator, asking only that he be given a vision as to the purpose of his existence. There is both humility and boldness in the petition. Few would stand in the light of Creation's candle, fearing that its brilliance would either blind or extinguish them. Few would chance to visit the dimension beyond death, knowing that return is often impossible.

The men spent the night looking up at the sky, where their sun was the star of others' worship. The clusters of twinkling dots had ancient names in more languages than were ever written, and they were yet being named again this night somewhere across eternity. "Oh the binding firmament that seems to house us all." That is the silent expression of those who gaze and try to make a unity of what they see and feel. It is a feeling difficult to bring into the light of day.

Anglo felt the awe of the night desert sky. He felt at peace. There were few thoughts bubbling to the surface to disturb his non-objective awareness. And yet he had the feeling that he would not go up on the hill as the sun set the next day. In his memory he could not recall how he had become committed to the vision quest. He remembered the preparations, but he could not remember why. It was as if he had put his foot into a running stream, whose undetected swiftness had spun him around and caused him to fall into its mercies. And now, carried into deeper water, he was out of control, going where its rapids dictated. If the waters deposited him at the base of the sacred hill, he did not know if he would have the strength to climb it.

The day dawned through the crags of the granite mountains and spilled into the desert valley

like molten manna. Anglo and White Wing were
in prayer to receive it. When full light gave
strength to their day, they went to work on the
final preparations for the sweatlodge and the
holy hill. They did the work without talking,
each man aware of how he worked in concert
with the other. White Wing did not have to ask
or motion Anglo to stand off the hill while he
placed the flags, spread the sage, and completed
the circle with the string of tobacco ties. Anglo
anticipated the right action and performed it before there was a need for prompting.

As the sun moved into the West, the men
waited in the shade of the campsite for the appointed time to light the fire under the seven
stones. Anglo laid out the contents of his medicine bag on his blanket and used each item as
the focus of a prayer for strength, courage, and
worthiness. White Wing sat away from him to
give him space. He tried to pray for Anglo but
his focus was not steady. He got to his feet,
and what began as a pace back and forth in the
sand of the wash turned into dance. White Wing
reverted to the form of worship that he knew
best.

The dance style was not the Fancy Dance for
which Dancer had made his reputation. It was
rather the slow, stately dance pattern that had
been taught by the Elders to have emanated
from the Ancient Ones. If the sands had memory, they had felt the pattern danced many times

in Petroglyph Canyon. It had been danced at Mesa Verde and Canyon de Chelly and in a thousand secret places where there was sacred ground. There was dance before there was language. The expression of worship was felt in the Earth, and the memory in the sands was blown in the winds of time from millennium to millennium, to collect under the feet of this man in this solitary place.

Anglo looked up from his medicine bag to watch White Wing dance. The beauty of it brought tears to his eyes. There was no audience here. The dancer was not seeking the praise of men. The body was not being exercised as much as it was being exorcised of imperfection. There was no drumbeat other than the heart. There was no singing other than the wind. But Anglo felt the power of White Wing's vibration as if it was a symphony in crescendo.

The hour came to light the fire and collect the canteens. The fire made a slight roaring as the chimney formed by the stacked wood caused a rushing of air. The flames flickered on the faces of the red sandstone, and the men could feel the reflection of the intense heat. When the wood collapsed into hot coals, the men undressed to nakedness. Anglo set the materials for the pipe ceremony inside the door of the lodge. White Wing entered the tipi, took his place to the South just inside the door, and filled the pipe as Anglo lit sweetgrass and shook it just outside. The pipe was then placed against the mound of the fire pit and White Wing accepted the seven stones as they were handed in on pitchfork-like sticks. A stone was carefully placed to the West side of the pit first, and then in order to the North, East and South. The final three stones were placed in the center. Each stone was touched with the chin of the pipe as it came in. A small piece of cedar was put on each of the first four stones to sweeten the lodge.

Anglo then entered the lodge with two canteens of water and an offering of tobacco ties. He moved South around White Wing and sat in the North where he secured the door flaps.

In the total darkness, White Wing poured the first water on the rocks and began the first of six spirit songs. As he completed each song he poured more water. The steam heat grew more intense with each pouring. Controlled breathing was necessary. Wiping the body with the sage seemed to relieve painful hot spots. Anglo sang a song in the Pueblo language which translated, "Grandfather have pity on me." Remaining in the sweatlodge required a high state of self-discipline.

At the end of the first round of songs and prayers, White Wing opened the door flap. The light revealed the two men soaked and glistening in their own sweat. Both men drank from one of the canteens to avoid dehydration and unconsciousness. Thus refreshed, they closed the flap and the steam process began again. This was the part of the ceremony set aside for personal prayers. White Wing, as the ceremonial leader, was supposed to start, but he remained silent after several pours of water to build up steam. Anglo did not break the silence.

The heat built up to high intensity before White Wing spoke.

"This is not your vision quest, is it?" he said out of the darkness.

Anglo replied without thought or rationalization. "No," he said.

"When did you know?" White Wing asked softly.

"Only in this moment," Anglo answered truthfully.

"This has been your purpose for being in Las Vegas."

"I see that now," Anglo said.

"I am ready," White Wing said. "Let us sing songs of joy and thanks, and then pray for me. I do not know what awaits."

The door to the sweatlodge was opened three additional times as the seven stones gave up their energy, and the men alternated between steamy darkness and the pale yellows and golds of afternoon. After the third opening, they smoked the pipe according to their devotion. For the first time in his traditional life, White Wing took four draws on the pipe before passing it to Anglo.

When the flaps were closed for the fourth time, the remainder of one canteen was poured on the cooler stones and the men prayed in silence in the moderate steam. The sun was setting and layers of pinks and violets began to spread across the western horizon. When they emerged, there would only be time enough to wash down with a canteen and whisk away the beads of water on their skin with the curved rib bone of a bighorn sheep. By the time White Wing had his last sip of water and walked to the hill, he would be dry. By the time Anglo handed White Wing his blanket and closed the circle behind him, the twilight would be coming into night. Before Anglo got out of sight, he turned to take a final look at the hill. White Wing was in silhouette against the sky of the evening star. He had already begun to dance.

CHAPTER THIRTY

The night was mild, but Anglo was physically and emotionally exhausted from the events of the day. He laid a small campfire to be lit in the morning chill and ate a cold supper of beef jerky, beans from a can, and salted crackers. The food tasted like an extravagant feast after his long fast. He drank two cups of water from the remains in the canteens, and although it was tepid and flat from storage, it too was satisfying. The water and the meal revived him enough to consider his new duties as White Wing's helper.

He removed the canvas from the tipi so that the quilt might dry out overnight. He could take the structure down in the morning and think about building his own lean-to against the rocks. He would also need to inventory the food and water supplies and ration his daily intake so that there would be plenty for White Wing when he came off the hill. White Wing would desperately need the water and then at least two meals before he could be expected to hike back to the trailhead. Being the helper was a serious responsibility. He would stay close to camp and pray for his tribal nephew.

Anglo wondered what White Wing was experiencing on the hill. After his day of intense preparation and his spiritual realization during the sweat, White Wing would probably dance himself into exhaustion and then, wrapped in his blanket, fall into his shelter for a long, deep sleep. Anglo thought these thoughts, but he did not want to allow them to flow into worry. He realized that he must have faith in White Wing's safety. No venomous creature would cross the barrier of tobacco ties. If Daniel of the Bible slept with lions, surely this Indian man called into Creation's service would remain unharmed.

In the lamentation that he had suffered in Red Rock Canyon, Anglo thought that he had cried out all the guilt of his past life, but he was troubled by a thought tainted by comparison. In his closeness to White Wing, he had begun to regard the younger man as his son. But the regard was shadowed by the fact of his own natural son, Theo, and of his daughter, Buffy, as well. The kinship that he felt for White Wing was stronger than the bond that he remembered for his own children. He had shared more, given more of himself to the Indian boy, than he had given to his own blood.

There was still a pocket of painful regret which persisted from his past life. It was an incompletion. How could he have considered himself prepared for the ordeal of the vision quest with such an incompletion? The void within would have become magnified on the hill. It would have made the quest a more dangerous undertaking. The sweat, the sage, and the sweetgrass smoke can only do so much to purify. The man himself is responsible for his mind, his thoughts, his fears, and his regrets. The mind itself, with its storehouse of false images, is the barrier to great vision.

Anglo smiled in acknowledgment of his pride in White Wing and of his regret concerning his own children. There was purpose in this night for both White Wing and himself. They had simultaneously served and been served by each other. Anglo's internal eyes, the core of his heart, had been opened to the potentials of his natural children. Why could he not serve them as well as he had served his Indian son? The warmth of the answer was felt as the closure of the internal void. Anglo rejoiced in it as a healing.

Far away, wherever Theo and Buffy were in Virginia, their father was already entering their spiritual hearts. He came instantaneously as he himself was healed, alone in the dark night of the wilderness. He came as invisible light that protected them from all things venomous in their lives. He came to restore them to himself, so that they might one day be able to face Creation alone on a sacred hill, free from all incompletions. He did not imagine how this would be accomplished, just as he had not known how he would serve White Wing when he came to Las Vegas. He did not have to plan. That he knew. What he had to do, however, was to reach out to them. Whatever occurred after that would be appropriate. Anglo wrapped himself in his blanket, laid down on the still warm sand, and slept a deep, dreamless sleep. It seemed to him that the reunion with his children had already been accomplished. His peace was complete.

The sun rose on the first day of the vision quest. It showed its light on two men sitting cross-legged, about half a mile from each other. Both were in prayer. Both had the thirst of a dry morning mouth, but only one could drink. One man began his day by improving his campsite and breaking a twelve-hour fast from his last meal. The other man shuffled in a slow dance step, which the Indians call Straight Dancing, around the three-quarter arc of a circle. His posture was dignified and erect. His face turned dramatically toward the four directions, and to the sky above and to the ground below his feet, as if he were expecting something to appear. He danced naked until the sun began to burn his skin and then he took shelter in a pit covered by a lean-to. He knew that he must endure, so he guarded his strength the way he would pace a painted pony across a trackless divide. From time to time, he would sing prayer songs in a very old language. But most of the day, he listened. He listened for something beyond his physical senses, for voices that he had never heard before.

The first twenty-four hours ended at sunset. One man ate a cold supper to satisfy his small hunger, and lit a campfire more for company than for warmth. He performed a solitary pipe ceremony and made a cornmeal offering to whatever spirits might be in the night to help and protect his son. The day had seemed long. Mostly he had stayed in the shade of the cliff which towered above his campsite. He had prayed even while collecting firewood and burying the ashes from the large fire which had heated the sweatlodge stones. He remained awake late enough to see the passage of the moon across the light, dimpled black canvas of the sky. There were few clouds on its face, so the coming of the next day promised to be hot.

The man on the hill saw the same moon and remained awake and alert until after sunrise. He spoke to the moon and to the familiar star formations. He asked the night itself to whisper its secrets. There was no response. His throat was parched and ached from beseeching. His mouth was dry and his lips were sore and encrusted. His stomach churned and was sometimes painfully near cramping. He took refuge from the sun and entered a fitful sleep in the bottom of his pit.

Twilight marked the end of the second day. White Wing had been told by the Elders who related the vision quest history of his tribe that the third day on the hill was the hardest. For in these hours the metabolism of the body changes. Energy no longer is available from the empty intestines, so the body desperately seeks nourishment from its own cells. The starvation reflex results in severe stomach and muscle cramps. A painful burning sensation is felt in many vital organs. Dehydration complicates the symptoms, and delirium and hallucination often result.

White Wing was not fighting the physical degradation. The growing pain in his joints, the wrenching of his gut, and his inability to generate enough spit to moisten his cracked lips were part of the price he thought he must pay to demonstrate worthiness. He was not disappointed that his vision had not come in the first two days. Great visions required great testing. He told himself that he would endure with dignity.

But the night spent in agony, alternating prayerful dances and fervent pleadings, brought no vision. Four times White Wing's devotion collapsed on the sage-strewn ground, and he lay in delirium. He lost any sense of how long he had succumbed to exhaustion. Nevertheless, each time he gathered the strength and the will to rise and continue.

At daybreak, sitting motionless in the dance-disturbed sand near the East edge of the circle, White Wing opened his eyes and looked into the face of a coyote watching him at a distance of less than twelve feet. He greeted Coyote in his native language, but the animal did not shy away. It continued to stare at White Wing. And then it laughed at him. The sound was high-pitched and staccato. Then Coyote shook its head as if to mock the pitiful man on the hill.

"You are filthy and only fit for turkey vultures," White Wing thought he heard coyote say. "Why do you starve yourself when you have a city full of food? You are a fool."

"Go home to your den, you trickster," White Wing said weakly with a wave of his arm, but Coyote held his ground.

"The scorpions will make a feast of you if you stay on this hill," Coyote taunted. "The one like you has water. He has food. Why don't you stop torturing yourself? Humans are so stupid. You embarrass us."

"I seek my vision," White Wing said in defense.

"My vision is a fat kangaroo rat who doesn't see me coming," Coyote mocked with another shrill laugh.

"You have come to test me," White Wing retorted.

"I thought I was doing you a favor." Coyote raised his head and looked away as if offended.

"You have favored me," White Wing said getting to his feet. "You have given me hope. For whom the spirits test, they shall also reward."

"You are beyond pity. I give up on you. I'll be back tomorrow for my share of your flesh. Don't say I didn't warn you."

White Wing watched Coyote arrogantly walk away, turning twice with a halting look over its shoulder to see if the man was still defiant. Then the animal broke into a trot and disappeared into the rocks.

CHAPTER THIRTY-ONE

When Anglo and Dancer had planned the vision quest for Anglo, the five days had been segmented into one day for preparation, three days to occupy the hill, and one day to recover. As the evening approached which ended White Wing's third day on the hill, Anglo anticipated the need for a fourth day. Dancer had warned him of the possibility. Unless White Wing completed his quest early on the fourth day and was able to travel, there was no way that the men could make the rendezvous with Sue and Debbie. The women would be disappointed—maybe even angry—that they had to return the next day, but they had been cautioned. Anglo trusted that they would not panic when he and Dancer failed to arrive on schedule. He did not want them sending out the Park Rangers.

Anglo regretted that he had not brought his hand drum. The drum would have been a comfort during the long days and nights of waiting. He could not find enough to do with his hands. He was restless and wanted to walk and explore, but his duty was to stay near the camp. By agreement, he was allowed to climb a ridge one time a day near sunset and take a brief long-distance view of the hill. If White Wing was ready to come off, he would signal by massing the ceremonial flags at the center of the circle. No signal was shown. White Wing could not be seen. Anglo assumed that he was sheltered in the pit.

From everything Anglo knew about the vision quest ceremony, the ritual he and White Wing were enacting was unorthodox. Neither of them possessed the knowledge or experience of a cacique or medicine man. Each man had been sincere in his effort, but Anglo wondered this night if their medicine was strong enough. What if White Wing suffered and endured with great courage and came away with no vision? At what point would Anglo intervene to save his son from harm or even death? Anglo attempted to substitute prayer for doubts, but his concern for White Wing persisted. He finally took an empty canteen and used it like a drum to tap out accompaniment for his Pueblo songs. He sang softly, late into the night, as a tonal fortress against fear.

On the hill, White Wing was in a stupor. After the punishing sun had set, he crawled out of his hole and sat pulling at his knees to remain upright. The terrible pain of hunger that had kept him at the bottom of his hole, locked in the fetal position all day had subsided, but he was almost too weak to stand. He knew that he had dreamed during the past three days, but he had no memory of the images. He remembered Coyote, however, in every detail. He heard coyote calls in the night, but they were not speaking to him. They had their private conversations with the moon.

But the moon was overcast. Some moments it was a halo of disbursed luminescence, and then it appeared briefly only to be concealed again by heavy dark clouds. There might be light rain this night, but the cold air riding the moon needed the energy of the sun to make thunderheads. In the morning the white clouds would gather, and the heat would rise from the desert plains and cause them to billow and swell to extravagant heights. They would churn and accumulate all day into gigantic masses over the mountaintops. And then they would darken and begin to rumble with inner turbulence until they blackened the northwestern skyline like a curtain. Finally, in the late afternoon they would erupt.

Some practitioners of the vision quest believe that rain is a bad omen while the candidate is on the hill. Other medicine men believe the opposite. White Wing was in no condition to carry out the debate. He was near the limit of his endurance. He would try to dance one more time during this night. He would push himself to remain conscious. There was no pride left in him.

He had allowed the hope of a grand vision to slip away. He was poised to accept any vision. He was an empty vessel waiting to be filled—a humble, unadorned vessel waiting to be used.

Anglo was happy to see the dawning of the day that he expected would see White Wing come off the hill. After the long wait, there were finally things that he could do. There was a meal to prepare to restore White Wing's energy after the four-day ordeal. Although Dancer would have been cooking in the original scenario, Anglo had done much of the food planning and purchasing. Pemmican, made from choke cherries and roast jerky pounded together and mixed with melted suet, was the traditional restorative food. Four of the egg-shaped balls of pemmican had been purchased from the Paiutes and stored in Anglo's haversack in a plastic bag. Anglo would serve the pemmican with cups of the freshest water, brought in five days before, as soon as White Wing was helped into camp. He would have to eat and drink in small increments so that his stomach would accept it.

The celebration meal would come a few hours later. Anglo would start the soup early in the afternoon, simmering chunks of dried buffalo until the meat was tender and a tasty stock was produced. Then he would add more water, dried beans, corn, and squash, and cook it over a slow fire into the night. The smell of it alone would brighten White Wing's face. Finally, Anglo planned to cook a cornmeal bread in the camp skillet just before the soup was served. Anglo found joy in the idea of such a meal, prepared out of a haversack of dry foods, utilizing only one pot and one skillet. He patted the sheath knife attached to his belt and felt a self-sufficiency he had never felt before.

The dawn for White Wing was much less auspicious. He was huddled at the bottom of his shelter pit without a vision or even a dream to console him. His senses were numb. He was not even capable of despair. Both his body and his mind had surrendered to death, and yet he did not have the energy to embrace it. All day, the sun was strong, into the afternoon, and White Wing could not open his eyes without being repulsed by its blinding glare.

The rumbling penetrated his stupor sometime in the mid-afternoon. It was a deep, heavy, continuous, rolling sound that made him restless. Then he remembered the dark clouds across the moon and knew that the storm was coming. Rainstorms in the drought-prone desert are both infrequent and spectacular events. White Wing suddenly had a strong impulse to greet the Thunder Beings. He used the impulse to fuel his betraying muscles and crawl out of the pit. He lay at the center of the circle and saw the black curtain of the storm approaching from the northwest.

Fingers of jagged lightning reached out of the blackness and cannons of booming thunder followed. He could see the strings of rain falling onto the gray mountains where they danced on the cliffs and then plunged headlong into the gorges and ravines. Already, miles away, there were raging torrents of muddy water inundating the desert washes.

Then the thunderheads crossed over into the valley. White Wing felt the temperature change as a cool wind swept over the hill. He could smell the rain although it was still miles away. He could see the dust devils throwing up yellow-gray walls of particles in the air. In one area the whirlwinds had picked up sandstone dust and the haze was red-gray in color. The wild winds preceded the cloudbursts and rolled up the valley in a dust storm that was quickly put to ground by the downpour which closely followed.

White Wing watched the unfolding of the storm in fascination, transfixed to the spot where he lay. The sun had disappeared and the day was shattered into shadowless gray. Then the wall of dust struck his position. His skin was sandblasted by the 60 mile-per-hour gusts, and he covered his head with his arms to protect his eyes and wormed himself into the ground. The ceremonial flags flapped so furiously that they cracked and snapped like fireworks. The lean-to tarp was ripped from its frame and flew away like a strange rogue bat. White Wing's blanket followed like another odd creature, bound to the ground by loping undulations. The next thing White

Wing felt was the pummeling of propelled rain-drops. They were cold and impacted his dry, abused skin painfully. The man instinctively raised one hand to protect the top of his head and moved the other to safeguard his genitals. The noise of the storm fractured what remained of his senses and the extreme exposure pushed his body into clinical shock. White Wing lost consciousness.

Anglo saw the approach of the storm, but he was more worried about his soup than his safety. He suspected that there might be a hard rain, but he had not lived long enough in the desert southwest to realize what it implied. Neverthe-less, Anglo was prudent in his preparations. He moved the quilt, his sleeping blanket, and other camp supplies that he didn't want to get wet onto the protected ledge above the campfire. He planned to move his pot of soup and himself under his lean-to until the storm passed. The worst part of it, he thought, would be that he would have to rebuild the cooking fire. He stacked wood for that purpose on the ledge too, which was about chest high and about eight feet across by two feet deep. The bushel-basket-sized niches in the rock around it had served as their campsite cache.

When the wind came, it funneled down the wash with a blast of sand. Anglo turned his back against the onslaught and lifted the covered pot of soup off the fire, as the wind scattered the burning wood and coals across the sands. The rocky escarpment of the campsite broke enough of the wind's velocity to leave Anglo's lean-to in place against the rockface, and he took himself and his pot of soup under its shelter. Looking up the wash, he saw the water creeping over the sand bottom before the rain got to his position. The tide was less than an inch deep when it forced him out of the lean-to and continued on its way past him. He took the soup pot to the ledge and was positioning it when he felt the water soak his boots. The depth was about two inches and the rushing water made a wake around his ankles. Anglo decided to climb onto the ledge just as the rain itself hit. The rim of the rockface above partially protected him from the storm's impact, but Anglo could judge by the weight of the downpour on his back and the pounding in his ears that it was serious. It took him a minute after attaining the ledge to move the camp gear aside so he could turn and sit with his back against the wall. What he saw alarmed him for the first time. A curtain of water like the backside of a waterfall fell from the cliff above, but he would not be soaked within the crevice. Beyond the waterfall the rain was so hard that visibility was limited to a few feet. Something shot past the ledge two feet below him, almost close enough to reach out and touch. Anglo recognized it as the canvas top to his lean-to. His focus went immediately to the brown, churning water. What had been inches a minute ago was now over two feet deep and rising. Seeing the uprooted bushes and other debris speeding by on the top of the torrent caused Anglo to gasp involuntarily for breath. The recognition came an instant later. Anglo understood that he was witnessing a flash flood.

He rationally examined the crevice that he occupied. There was no place to climb beyond the narrow ledge. Instinctively he drew up his knees and pressed himself into the rock wall. The roaring river and pounding rain were louder than the thunder. He could not hear the lapping sound as the edge of muddy water reached the level of the ledge. Anglo was too paralyzed to attempt to save his soup when the flood overturned the pot and spilled its contents into the swirling abyss. Then the quilt and his blanket were swept away. Next, the heavier haversacks were spun around and sucked into the rapids. The water tugged at Anglo's feet and wet his bottom. He braced himself against the wall, but there were no hand holds to offer purchase. In the last seconds, as he fought to retain his perch against the impersonal onslaught, he recalled being Winn in the rapids of the French Broad River on a Smoky Mountain vacation in North Carolina. He had taken the family on a whitewater rafting trip and the rubber boat had overturned. What had the instructor said? Yes. Relax. Lie on your back with your feet in the direction of the flow.

Bounce off the rocks with your feet. Go with the current until you are carried into calm waters.

The thoughts were timely and useful, but they did not prevent Anglo from screaming as the water wrenched him from safety and cast him into the flood.

CHAPTER THIRTY-TWO

He thought he heard the tingling of old-time hawk bells, as if someone in ceremonial regalia had passed. He was aware that his naked body was dry and that he was free from pain. He opened his eyes. His cheek was against the damp sand and his ground-level view was of a desert tortoise, a foot from his nose, eating the egg-shaped fruit of a prickly pear cactus. The wrinkles and folds of its thick, elephant-like legs dominated White Wing's limited horizon. He elevated himself on his elbow and noticed the patches of new green grass that had sprouted on the hill. A 400-pound burro, half the size of a horse, was feeding on the grass. A fence lizard rolled in the sand beneath the burro as if to scratch its back, and White Wing could see the bright blue patches on its stomach.

He turned his head slowly, and was dumbfounded to see the hill occupied by what seemed to be a multitude of desert creatures. A gambel's quail, with its top-knot feathers prominent, crossed the muzzle of a rusty gray coyote, but the predator did not pounce. He seemed content to scratch his furry white belly.

There was no wind or rain on the hill, and the sun provided bright light from a hole in the sky directly overhead. Nevertheless, the dark wall of the storm surrounded the hill and there was no visibility beyond fifteen yards in any direction. White Wing surmised that the sacred hill was in the eye of the violent storm, and that the desert creatures had found it as a refuge from lightning and flash floods. They were perhaps in shock. It was his only explanation for their behavior, because surely the brown prairie falcon should have eaten the long-tailed kangaroo rat, and the burrowing owl was the natural enemy of the antelope ground squirrel—a chipmunk-sized meal with white lines running down each side of its gray body. But the falcon preened and the yellow-eyed owl only bobbed up and down reflectively, while their prey acted unconcerned.

Desert plants have remarkable regenerative potentials when inspired by rain. A dormant plant can literally flower in an hour. White Wing accepted the grass that the large blacktail jackrabbit was nibbling as part of this phenomenon, as he did other tasty food stuffs on which other creatures fed. A white-throated canyon wren was pecking at the seeds from severed stalks of Indian rice grass. There was a scorpion using its pincers to test the fruits blown from the strawberry hedgehog cactus. A black and tan horned lizard lay nearby, ignoring the ants who were also attracted to the sweet fruit. A roadrunner, impressive with its long tail and bill and bushy headcrest, was playing with string bean-looking things that White Wing recognized as sweet pods from a mesquite tree. A four-inch long tarantula, with its brownish-black hairy body and legs, was curious but unafraid. As White Wing completed his visual survey of the hill, he also identified a gila monster, formidable in its patterned black and yellow beadlike scales, and a sidewinder, a distinctive tan snake with eye flaps resembling horns, that felt no need to activate its rattle.

The presence of the venomous creatures did not threaten White Wing, and although the hill seemed crowded, there was a sense of calm. He was, however, not inclined to change his position other than to sit up and cross his legs for support. His feeling of amazement was still dominant, and it escalated to wide-eyed disbelief as a large bighorn sheep ram trotted through the black-gray storm wall and came onto the hill. The animal was grayish-brown with a white rump. It showed a huge set of curled horns. From the number of distinctive growth rings on the horns, it was evident that the ram was very old. Other creatures moved to make a path for the bighorn, and he walked directly to White Wing and stood before him—almost eye-to-eye—at a distance of about three feet. White Wing was shocked when it spoke to him in his own native language.

"Your Grandfathers have heard you."

The ram seemed to wait for White Wing to believe that he had spoken. "They say to you, 'Feed the people. Walk in a sacred manner across the land and there will be plenty. The Thunder Beings are your kin. Dance this dance and they will bring rain to your fields. Dance this dance and they will bring healing.'"

The ram shifted his weight to the hind legs and began to dance with his front hooves. He repeated the steps three times and then waited until White Wing got to his feet. The ram backed away to give space to the man and then repeated the steps. White Wing tried to keep in step with his own feet. His skill was excellent and his dance memory keen. The ram repeated the dance again and White Wing was synchronous in movement with him. Then, as if to test him, the ram lowered his massive head and stared at White Wing's feet until he repeated the dance solo. The bighorn shook his entire body in satisfaction and then turned and trotted off the hill and through the storm wall. Like a real Indian, the bighorn had not announced his leaving. He had made his presence. He required no further recognition.

White Wing stood at the center of the circle, staring at the place where the bighorn had disappeared, when he heard the flapping of huge wings above his head. A great golden eagle was descending through the blue circle of the open sky. It was brown with a white tailband and feathered legs. It was the most sacred creature in the pantheon of animal spirits. The eagle landed six feet from where White Wing stood in frozen awe. The bird walked on talons as large as a man's hands. Its body was three feet long. It stopped in front of White Wing just as he sank to his knees.

The voice that came out of the eagle was commanding. "You shall walk in a sacred manner." The eagle waited for a response.

"I will walk in a sacred manner," White Wing affirmed.

"You shall honor the ancient ways," the bird commanded.

"I will honor the ancient ways," White Wing responded.

"Take this feather as a symbol of your promise and your power." Saying this, the eagle extended his right wing, plucked out a tall, perfect feather with its powerful beak, and extended it to White Wing.

White Wing, still on his knees, accepted the feather from the eagle's beak. He held the bloody quill in both hands and raised it aloft, as the eagle ascended with powerful strokes of its wings that White Wing felt as wind on his face. He watched the eagle until it was a speck on the blue circle of the sky, and then it was gone.

White Wing fell from his knees to the sand, cradling the feather. He knew that it must never touch the ground. The sunlight on the hill became dim and gradually turned into night. He could see the stars in a circular window on the sky high above his head. In the darkness, he could not see his fellow creatures on the hill. His eyelids were heavy and sleep overcame him.

When Anglo was first sucked off the rock ledge into the raging flash flood, he was tumbled under the surface and carried wildly for a long distance. The gritty water served to blind him, and he struggled helplessly to the limit of his breath before popping to the top of the rapids. Gasping for air, he flailed against the tide amid rolling driftwood and uprooted cacti and bushes of all types. Although Anglo, as Winn, had learned to swim in the Chesapeake Bay and had experienced ocean undertow at Virginia Beach, his skill was useless against the force of the flood. There was no possibility of swimming across the flow in the deep gully that formed the wash.

Suddenly Anglo's right arm struck a submerged boulder in the path of the flood. The blow stunned him and he lost his tenuous hold on the surface and tumbled underwater again. His right arm was useless in the desperate attempt to regain the surface. It seared with pain and shocks of agony as the raging waters exacerbated the broken bone. Anglo was functioning on survival reflex. There was no panic, although his body railed against the threat of drowning. The violent moments were measured in seconds on the clock, but for Anglo the events were in slow motion. He reached across his body with his left arm to catch the wounded right arm and save it from further damage by holding it close to his body. As his lungs were about to expire and take in water instead of air, Anglo was able to align his body feet-first with the flow. The current supported him like a log and propelled him to the surface. He swallowed water in waves that broke over his face, but he was able to breathe.

Although he could not see ahead, he felt that the onrush of the makeshift river had slowed. In actuality, it had focused most of its energy in the narrows of the ravine, where rock cliffs and deep gullies made it run its course through a desert trough. Now nearing the end of its run, the flood spread out like a fan and was absorbed into the broader plain until it became an inch of creeping tide that petered out in the sand.

The thunderheads had passed and the rain had stopped. Anglo felt his behind bump on the bottom of the wash as it expanded into a kind of desert delta that would deposit him and rocks, and plant debris, and dozens of small drowned animals in its wake. The momentum of the flood would carry him no further. He sat up in the subdued water as it swirled around him. The darkness of the storm was already giving way to light. In the West, Anglo could see the sun, restored and sliding down into the gold shades which led to twilight.

Anglo sat holding his broken arm until the water around him had dissipated completely. He could see no identifiable landmarks. He could not estimate how many miles the river had carried him. He trusted that White Wing would have survived the storm on the high ground of the hill, but after his ordeal he would need food and, ironically, water. But the soup was gone. The canteens, everything was carried away by the flood. Anglo tried to get to his feet but did not have the strength. He noticed for the first time that one of his boots was missing, and the sock as well. The lost boot would make a good shade shelter for scorpions. It was somewhere out there in the broad flood plain. Anglo hoped to find it, and perhaps one of the canteens. He had his duty to White Wing. He would walk with the bare foot if necessary.

But, oh, the arm ached terribly. The bone had not punctured the skin, and Anglo was able to pull up the wet shirt sleeve enough to see the site of the injury. A bloody wound was at the center of a large, reddish-purple bruise on the forearm. The elbow seemed injured as well. Anglo lay down on his left side and supported the injured arm against his chest. He meant only to rest for a few minutes before attempting to find his way back to the campsite, but he lapsed into unconsciousness. Night came and he did not awake.

CHAPTER THIRTY-THREE

Debbie was running late. She had volunteered to make the picnic supper for Ramon and his uncle, but the preparations took longer than she expected. Then she could not find her video camera and when she did, she didn't have any unused tape cassettes.

"I had to get tape, didn't I?" Debbie said in excuse.

Sue was not pleased. "Dale Earnhart couldn't get us to the Valley of Fire on time. They will think that we forgot them."

Neither woman had consulted the Weather Channel, or they would not have been so surprised to see the dark storm front spread across the valley as they passed North Las Vegas on I-15. Twenty miles out into the barren landscape they encountered the heavy rain and the violent display of the thunderheads. The day turned dark and the driving wind and rain reduced visibility to the length of the car. Sue had no choice but to pull off the highway and wait out the storm.

"Every time the lightning flashes," Debbie said

to relieve the tension, "I imagine that God is taking my picture."

Normally, Sue would have responded with a caustic comeback designed to make Debbie laugh, but her thoughts were preoccupied. "The boys must be catching hell about now," she said soberly.

"Not to worry," Debbie responded. "They are Indians, aren't they? What's a rainstorm to them?"

"This is not your average thunderstorm," Sue said. "The last time I saw anything like this, we had a flash flood in Vegas that stacked cars like dominos in two or three casino parking lots."

"Oh, yeah, I remember that. Who would have believed it?"

"Well, believe it. It could be dangerous out there. Look at all that lightning."

"Indians know about that kind of stuff. The boys are probably real cozy in a cave somewhere, probably worrying about us."

"And well they should," Sue continued in seriousness. "We could get rear-ended by a sixteen-wheeler pulling off the highway. Or if we stopped too close to a bridge across a wash, a flood could come up and carry us away."

The rain continued to pound the car and gusts of strong wind rocked it. The women and the vehicle shivered with each violent gust. The girls were silent for some minutes before Debbie spoke.

"Let's sing some hymns."

Sue turned towards her in mock disgust. "What do you think this is, the Titanic?"

"No," Debbie replied sheepishly. "But it can't hurt."

"I'd rather sing some rock and roll. At least it would change the dead-man-walking mood we're in."

"Let's sing a Beatles song," Debbie suggested. "She loves you, yeah, yeah, yeah."

"That's perfect," Sue replied with a sarcastic smile. "If we pretend that God is a woman, *She Loves You* can be as good as a hymn."

The frightened women sang rock and roll standards for which they knew the lyrics for over half an hour, and then the hard rain abated, the sky lightened, and they were able to proceed down the highway.

As they approached the exit to the Valley of Fire, they could see the flashing lights of an emergency vehicle parked on the road near the Paiute Indian store. When they got to the vehicle, they saw that it was a Park Ranger patrol car blocking the road to the park. An officer in a hooded, two-piece yellow rainsuit came to Sue's window. The rain was still moderate although the wind had died down.

"Sorry, ladies," the officer said as soon as Sue had lowered the window, "the Park road is closed due to flash floods."

Sue casually extended her right hand and tapped Debbie's thigh to keep her quiet.

"When do you think you will reopen?" she asked.

"You might want to call the Visitor Center tomorrow if you plan to come out. My guess is noon or later. We will probably have to do some road work after we check things in the morning."

Sue thanked the officer and maneuvered the car into the Paiute store parking lot.

"Damn, what are we going to do now?" Sue seemed to be questioning herself. "Even if we tell the Ranger that the boys are camping, they can't do anything until morning."

"I vote that we keep our promise not to tell on the boys and come back tomorrow like we agreed," Debbie said with confidence.

"I guess we have no choice." Sue put the car in gear and headed back to the interstate.

"Do you think my sandwiches will keep until tomorrow?" Debbie asked. Sue did not respond. She was too troubled by the day to hear on the first asking.

The night was oblivious to White Wing. He did not remember crawling into the rain-eroded pit, or partially covering his nude body with sand as protection against the chill. He only woke when the glare of daylight brought him back into the world. He turned his head into the shadow of the pit to adjust his eyes, and saw the eagle feather positioned in the cavity of his chest. His first reaction was that a great bird must have been caught up in the whirlwinds of the storm and lost its feather in the struggle. Then he remembered his vision. The blood had dried at the base of the quill. For White Wing it was tangible proof of his experience. But he realized that the story could not be told to everyone. He would tell Anglo, and Joseph, and the tribal Elders who kept the old ways. They could help him to understand the vision. But he would not tell the unbelievers. His vision was a sacred trust. His heart pounded with the joy he felt at this realization, and its surge of energy enabled him to climb out of the pit and raise the holy eagle feather to the sun.

Then he surveyed the hill. All evidence of the vision quest was gone. He regretted the loss of the flags for he had intended them as a gift for Anglo. But where was Anglo? The question engendered a series of thoughts that exploded into White Wing's consciousness. He knew that the wash where they had made their camp would have flooded. Would Anglo have read the weather signs and moved the camp to high ground? Experienced explorers made their camps on the flat sand floors of washes for convenience and shade, but they were always watchful for the infrequent thunderstorms that posed flash flood danger. A tenderfoot like Anglo might not understand the vulnerability of his campsite.

White Wing came off the hill in a stumbling run. He was hampered by weakness and a pain-

inhibited body, but he ran striding with the eagle
feather in his right hand. He crossed a ridge of
boulders and climbed down into the wash. The
raging flood had passed through, uprooted every
plant, and swept along every loose rock in its
path. White Wing hurried down the gully as fast
as his feeble body would carry him, until he
came to the rocky cliff and ledge that had been
their campsite. It, too, had been swept clean.
White Wing cried out Anglo's Indian name and
the sound echoed off the cliff walls. He called
out and then listened. Called out and listened.
He tried to whistle but his cracked lips could
not instrument the effort. In exhaustion and
hopelessness he collapsed on the sand. For a moment he convulsed in torment, his body shaking,
his throat gripped, his eyes too dry to form
tears. Then he calmed himself. He brought his
breathing back into a regular cycle. He lifted the
eagle feather up in front of his face, and he
prayed for strength to search for Anglo.

Anglo woke to a series of short, high squeals
from a prairie falcon. The falcon and a hissing
turkey vulture were nearby, debating the owner-
ship of a ground squirrel drowned in the flood.
When Anglo adjusted his eyes to the glaring sunlight, he became aware of additional scavenger
groupings on the flood plain, arguing over other
carcasses. The crossing shadow of a large bird
caused Anglo to turn his attention above his

head. He counted four turkey vultures in a pattern apparently centered on him.

Painfully, he got to his knees to assure the vultures that he was still alive. His injured arm was misshapen by swelling and hideously discolored in shades of purple and blue. The wound throbbed with the beats of his heart. Anglo inspected the rest of his body and found numerous cuts, scrapes, and bruises. His pants and shirt were torn or ripped in many places. His hair was full of sand, as if he had body-surfed onto the beach at Virginia Beach, except that the sand was less coarse and was reddish. He felt three sizable knots on his head that were painful when touched, and perhaps matted with a little blood. When he tried to stand, he discovered that the ankle on his naked foot was sprained. He tested it to make sure it was not broken, and then he sat back down.

He judged that he was in very poor shape to fulfill his responsibility to White Wing, but he was determined to try. If the flood had washed his carcass and those of the dead animals into this area, perhaps the canteens and the haversacks were carried here as well. Without water and food, Anglo concluded that he would be of little help to White Wing. First he would search for a tall stick to use as a cane. There was much driftwood debris nearby in which to begin the search. The stick might also be needed to fend off the vultures, should he fall and not be able to get up. The sheath knife had remained on his belt due to a good handle strap and snap. That was a plus. But Anglo could not see himself in a knife fight with the sharp-beaked, long-necked vultures.

By the position of the sun, Anglo thought that it must be after nine o'clock. By this hour, White Wing had been without food or water for more than four and a half days. Anglo would have to hurry. First, find a suitable stick for support, and then make a limping survey of the general area for a canteen or one of the supply sacks. He must find something quickly, not only for White Wing's survival, but also for his own. Find something to keep them alive, and then hobble, if he could, up the wash until he found the landmark cliff where the camp had been. From there he would rush to the hill to help his son. Anglo felt for his medicine bag and gripped it with both hands in a prayer for strength to save White Wing. Then he struggled to his feet and began.

CHAPTER THIRTY-FOUR

The air was fresh, even crisp, from the cleansing rain and the remnants of the cold front from Canada. The high temperature of this day would be about 80 degrees. The sky was azure and almost cloudless.

White Wing stumbled down the wash in his nakedness, looking as primitive as the first native who had ever walked in this desert. He did not know how far the wash extended or what he would find at its end. His body was fueled by purpose that denied the frailties of the flesh. But even inspiration has limitations. It can force the body beyond endurance, but when the body finally falls, it is not then able to get back up. It risks life itself toward a distant, often impossible goal. It courts death by obsessive will.

If freed from the single focus of finding Anglo, White Wing would have found a large, sharp-edged rock and cut into a barrel cactus. He would have sucked the moisture out of its watery pulp to survive. He would have found a path back to the trailhead, gathering strength along the way by eating whatever the desert plants offered. But White Wing did not consider survival without Anglo.

The stick was a good one. As tall as the staff of Moses, it supported Anglo in his search in the wilderness as it had the enlightened Hebrew's. Anglo went unsteadily, haltingly, from debris pile to debris pile, surveying the ground in between for needful things. Once at a pile, he planted his feet and used the stick to search through the tangle of uprooted bushes and storm trash for anything recognizable.

The broken limb was too painful to be allowed to dangle at his side, so Anglo put the arm inside his shirt and supported it by buttoning above and below. Since the bare foot and ankle sprain were on the same side as the broken arm, the left arm and leg had to be relied on to do the work of the search.

He saw the strap tangled in the blackened branches of tumbleweed in the fifth pile of debris that he inspected. The canteen itself was partially buried in sand and loose rock deposited by the flood. He fell to his knees and dug at the treasure with his only useful hand. It came free and he held it. It felt light. He shook it. There was water in it, but perhaps no more than a cup. At least it was something. It could have been one of the canteens already emptied.

Anglo looked at the canteen for a long moment.

He was thirsty. He was tempted to drink the contents in hopes of finding another canteen, perhaps a full one. No, he decided. The water was for White Wing. He slung the canteen over his left shoulder and resumed his search. The scavengers in his path raised their wings and hopped a few yards away, but as soon as Anglo passed, they went immediately back to their meals. Other vultures and hawks circled in the clear sky above.

A strip of color led Anglo to his sleeping blanket. An edge of the blanket protruded out of the sand enough to catch his attention. He tugged with his one good arm, but had to dig on his knees to finally retrieve it. Part of the blanket was still wet and muddy. It was too heavy to shake out with one hand. He placed it over his left shoulder as well as he could, one end dragging in the sand. He could not help that. As the sun dried the blanket it would become lighter and easier to shake out.

Now Anglo considered how long he should continue to search for more water and the missing food before leaving the area to find White Wing. The position of the sun told him that he had been occupied for more than an hour. The labor had seemed much longer. He had had to rest after examining the last two debris piles before he was able to proceed. Heavier objects, like the full canteens and the haversacks, might have fallen out of the flood sooner than a near-empty canteen or a blanket. Anglo narrowed his search area based on this deduction. He also felt that he was becoming better able to read the debris signs as to where the flood had flowed.

An exhausting hour later he found the haversack. It was partially buried in sand, but there was evidence that it had come to rest like a stone slab while the remaining tide had flowed around it. The straps were still tightly in place. The canvas bag had been Army issue in World War II. Its once-dark green color had faded long ago, but its durable construction had kept it in use. The find seemed a miracle to Anglo. The sack contained both his and Ramon's wallets, but the most important item was the plastic bag full of pemmican. The crackers and other dried foods were ruined by the water that soaked into the bag, but it did not matter. The rich fruit sugar and meat protein of the pemmican was enough. Anglo removed one of the egg-shaped delicacies and ate to restore his energy. He took a mouthful, began to chew, and then stood to arrange the sack, canteen, and blanket for walking. He chewed and swallowed as he walked. His euphoria carried him with a strength that his injured ankle could not deny. He pointed himself toward the mouth of the wash and hobbled forward with determination and urgency.

White Wing rounded the final bend in the wash and looked out onto the flood plain. Three hundred yards into the desert a strange apparition was coming towards him. It had a halting, one-sided gait and a single wing that draped from its shoulder and dragged behind it in the sand. Its head was down, concentrating on its progress. It was a left-sided creature, its upper body seemingly void of a right appendage. In the glare of the sun, in his desperate condition, White Wing could not put a name to it. He wondered if it was another aspect of his vision. He shaded his eyes with his hand and concentrated on the image from a kneeling position. Suddenly he knew, and he attempted to cry out but was unable to get more than a croaking sound from his parched throat. He got to his feet and pushed forward, waving his arms for attention.

Anglo looked up to take a bearing on the mouth of the wash and saw White Wing frantically lurching toward him. He dropped the blanket and haversack off his shoulder and closed the gap between them as rapidly as he was able. They fell into each other's arms and then sank to their knees, still in the embrace. After a few moments of reassurance that the reunion was real, they sat back in the sand and appraised each other. Each was emotionally distressed at the other's appearance, not realizing in that moment that he, himself, appeared to have narrowly survived the ordeal.

Anglo extended the canteen to White Wing, who took it willingly. As he unscrewed the cap,

White Wing could discern from the sand grit in the grooves that the canteen had not been opened since the flood. Anglo had not drunk from the canteen, but had saved the water for him. He was very moved by the discovery, but did not want to compromise Anglo's sacrifice with emotion. In the tribal council he would relate this fact in his recounting of these days. The Elders would thunder their rattles and raise their eagle feather fans in honor when they heard of this sacrifice, but the only honor now was the simple acceptance of the gift. White Wing took slow sips of the warm, stale water. It was more than wonderful. It was life.

"I have found the pemmican," Anglo told him.

The emotion was more than White Wing could contain, and he somehow summoned a wail of joy and a few tears of gratitude.

An hour later they had moved into the wash and found a shady place to rest and eat the pemmican. When White Wing felt better, he used Anglo's knife to cut an arm sling from the blanket for Anglo's arm, and a breech-cloth and serape for himself.

"We must get to the trailhead before the girls leave us," White Wing said. "We cannot stay another day here. You must get to a hospital before the arm gets infected."

The trailhead was a journey of about five miles, but it had to be taken in easy stages. Once they stopped when White Wing found a barrel cactus. It was the first water Anglo had drunk since the flood. He didn't mind that it came drops at a time and had a peculiar flavor.

Sue and Debbie got to the park three hours prior to their scheduled rendezvous with Ramon and Uncle Booker. There had been two places on the narrow, two-lane highway into the park where they had to stop while road crews worked to make it passable. Flash floods had obscured the roadway with heavy deposits of sand and rocks.

When they reached the trailhead, they nervously searched the picnic area for signs of the men, but were disappointed.

"What if they don't come by three?" Debbie asked.

"Then we wait until dark," Sue answered.

"And what if they still don't come?"

"Then we have a problem."

"We'll have to tell the Rangers," Debbie insisted. "I don't care what we promised. I can't go on like this."

"I know it's hard," Sue admitted, swallowing the anxiety in her throat.

"If they die out there, I will never forgive them," Debbie said with tears in her eyes.

"They won't die," Sue said to comfort her. "They are Indians. You said so yourself."

"Ramon is an Indian. His uncle is a pretend Indian," Debbie corrected.

"Maybe Uncle Booker was a boy scout," Sue said to be positive.

The hours that they waited were difficult. There was plenty of food, and a cooler full of drinks on ice, but they were only interested enough to satisfy their thirst with a couple of diet soft drinks. Most of the time they stayed in the shade and took turns sitting at a picnic table, or pacing to and from the road to look down the White Domes trail for the men.

Debbie saw them first and screamed. Sue ran from the picnic table to the trailhead, where Debbie stood in frozen disbelief. Sue, too, was stopped in her tracks by the dreadful appearance of the men. They were so unlike the men who had begun the trip as to be unrecognizable.

Debbie continued to lament, "Oh, my God" over and over until Sue broke into a run, and then she followed. Up close, the men were in even worse condition than the distant view indicated. Their beautiful fellow performer was emaciated, filthy and seemingly a step away from total collapse. If his eyes had not been so radiant, he might have passed for a crudely dressed corpse. Uncle Booker was obviously in worse condition. Although he still had his clothes, they were nothing more than rags. The stress of pain contorted his dirty face, and without the support of Ramon and the long stick, he surely could not have stood, let alone walked. The arm sling cradled an arm so gruesomely swollen that the shirt had been ripped apart to accommodate it. The wound was almost black and it reeked with an offending odor. Both women gasped at the sight of it and wept more tears. Their emotions were a complex mix of joy at seeing the men and despair over their condition.

"We've got to get you to a hospital," Sue reasoned.

"Water," Anglo said weakly.

Debbie ran back to the car as the other three made further progress along the trail. She returned with two cans of cold sodas.

"Go slow," Ramon warned.

Sue held one can for Anglo to drink from while Dancer helped himself to the other. Both men managed smiles of gratitude. The drinks gave them the energy to be helped to the car.

During the ride to the emergency room at Sunrise Hospital, Anglo and Dancer each ate a sandwich in small bites and drank more fluids. On arrival, both men were treated for dehydration and shock. Dancer did not want to be admitted to the hospital, but Sue and the emergency room staff insisted. Anglo had x-rays taken of his arm and foot, and was soon sent upstairs for specialized treatment of his broken, putrefactive arm.

Dancer was released from his hospital bed the next morning and joined the girls at Anglo's bedside, but the older man was unable to do much more than acknowledge them. Dancer came close to the bed and whispered into his ear, "The eagle feather is real. The vision is true. Get well so that we can smoke the pipe again."

Sue insisted that Ramon recover at her house. He slept for most of the next three days, only getting up for meals. When Sue or Debbie was not caring for him, their housemaid was hired as a temporary nurse.

Sue passed the word to the Folies production staff that Ramon had been hospitalized and was recovering from an accident. She told them that he did not plan on returning to the show. The Folies went on with Ramon's substitute, a chorus dancer thrilled to continue as the featured performer in the Native Fever act. He did not earn the spontaneous ovations that accompanied Ramon's performances, but the audiences never knew what they were missing. At the Tropicana, a cast change in the Folies show was considered business as usual.

Sue and Debbie had not missed a scheduled performance during the eventful weeks with Ramon and Uncle Booker, but their jobs were little on their minds. Dancer had tried to satisfy their curiosity with details of the flash flood and the search and reunion with Anglo, but he did not allude to the vision quest. From their point of view, Ramon could not successfully explain how Indians could be caught so unaware in a dangerous storm. Sue and Debbie continued to speculate privately about what really occurred.

They suspected that it was something secret and ceremonial that had them so occupied that they did not reckon the danger.

"Maybe they were eating those cactus buttons that make you high," Debbie suggested.

"It's called peyote. It's mescaline. It will give you hallucinations," Sue said. "I don't think Ramon uses it. He couldn't dance every night like he does if he was using anything. He'd spin right off the stage and fall into the pit."

"Well, what was with that feather?" Debbie asked. "He was holding onto it like it was the Holy Grail."

"So he found a feather. It was probably an eagle feather. Nobody touches an Indian's eagle feather. You ought to know that by the way Ramon treats his costume. You don't mess around with his eagle feathers."

"Well, whatever they did out there, I hope that it was worth it," Debbie concluded. "It almost killed them."

CHAPTER THIRTY-FIVE

The news came to Joseph on the feet of Carlos, who had been told by Dancer's mother that he was ready to return to the reservation. Dancer had telephoned his mother at the restaurant where she worked and told her no more than to get the message to Carlos. She had waited until the end of her workday to stop at the Silva's home and speak the message. Carlos had then waited until morning to see Joseph at the cacique's wall.

Joseph had waited patiently for many months to receive this news. He might have sent Carlos to determine the status of Anglo's mission after the first or second month, but doubt was inappropriate. Now that the boy himself had sent the message, Joseph saw it as an especially good omen. When Anglo and White Wing returned to the pueblo, they would say what needed to be said. Perhaps what they had to tell could only be shared in the kiva. That would be a great event for the Elders. It would require serious preparation. Joseph found himself smiling in anticipation of the event. He recalled the happiness Anglo had brought with his spirit. Now that Anglo had completed his mission, Joseph considered sponsoring him for a warriors' society. Joseph would give one of his own eagle feathers to Anglo, and the chief warrior society veteran would paint symbols on Anglo's face. Then and forever, at the Corn Dance and the Animal Dance, Anglo would wear his eagle feather and his warrior paint and all people would know him as a worthy man.

Carlos collected gifts of food for the trip to Las Vegas. Maria and White Wing's mother made generous contributions. It was a happy day, and Joseph made a special prayer and offering for a safe trip before Carlos drove off the reservation.

In Las Vegas, Anglo was out of the hospital and recovering in Sue's guest room. Dancer remained as a recovering guest, too, but was moved to the sofa bed in the living room.

Dancer humorously warned his father-uncle about the food. "They will try to feed you six times a day. If we eat everything they serve us, we will become too fat to Straight Dance."

The day came when Carlos arrived. Although Anglo and White Wing were clean, groomed, and normally dressed, he was still shocked by their appearance and injuries. His eyes asked many questions, but he was too polite to pose them in the presence of the white women. Finally, White Wing took his cousin out of the house and said the only words that would cause him to wait longer for the appropriate time and place.

"There has been a vision quest."

Carlos felt his jaw drop. Then the word 'who' became written on his facial expression.

"Me," White Wing affirmed. "Father Anglo was my spirit guide and helper."

Carlos could not resist a sympathetic comment to his oldest friend and tribal brother. "Tough quest," he said with a sincere smile.

"Tough quest," White Wing agreed and then he embraced his brother until the trembling of their mutual emotion passed.

On the final morning in Las Vegas, five people sat in the ceremony of welcoming the sun. The Indians sang prayer songs, and when light filtered onto the courtyard of Sue's home, the pipe was passed and everyone smoked.

"You are always welcome at our pueblo," Dancer assured Sue and Debbie.

"This invitation is not given lightly," Anglo added.

"I know," Sue said. "The same goes out to you wherever we are. We're not sure how long we will stay in Las Vegas. The life here seems a bit shallow right now."

"We're going to see you in Santa Fe," Debbie promised. "A few months from now we're going to wonder if this really happened. The only way to make sure will be to see if you exist. We'll have to see you again to prove that we are sane."

"Come as my sisters," Dancer said.

"Come as my daughters," Anglo added.

The leave-taking was emotional for the girls. While final hugs and kisses were exchanged, Carlos waited at the wheel of the pick-up truck that he and Dancer had loaded with Dancer's and Anglo's personal things from the apartment. The morning was still early when they pulled away and turned a corner that took them out of sight.

The trip back to Santa Fe was long. Sitting three across in the cab of the truck, the brims of their cowboy hats almost touching, the three men looked like day laborers on their way to work. Anglo did not complain, but the boys knew that his arm would ache miserably, medicine or no, after a few hours of travel in the truck. Dancer had a pocketful of large bills, and he planned to treat them to a good motel and restaurant meal when they stopped early in the afternoon when the heat and dust became oppressive. They would stop often to stretch Anglo's sensitive ankle and to drink something. There was no hurry. They had no obligations in the world. There were no happier men on its highway.

ABOUT THE AUTHOR

Monty Joynes is a career consumer magazine editor and publisher, beginning with *Metro Magazine* and concluding with *Holiday*, the national travel magazine. He has co-authored five titles in the *Insiders' Guide* series and two produced film scripts. *Naked Into the Night* was the first book in the "Anglo" series, and the third book in the series, *Save the Good Seed*, will be published in 1999. Monty and wife Pat live in Boone, North Carolina.